the Devil's Chair

BASED ON THE CASSADAGA LEGEND

KEITH ROMMEL

HELLBENDER BOOKS

an imprint of Sunbury Press, Inc.
Mechanicsburg, PA USA

an imprint of Sunbury Press, Inc.
Mechanicsburg, PA USA

For information about special discounts for bulk purchases, please contact Sunbury Press Orders Dept. at (855) 338-8359 or orders@sunburypress.com.

To request one of our authors for speaking engagements or book signings, please contact Sunbury Press Publicity Dept. at publicity@sunburypress.com.

FIRST HELLBENDER BOOKS EDITION: September 2025

Set in Adobe Garamond Pro | Interior design by Crystal Devine | Cover design by Lawrence Knorr | Edited by Sarah Peachey.

Publisher's Cataloging-in-Publication Data
Names: Rommel, Keith, author.
Title: The devil's chair : based on the Cassadaga Legend / Keith Rommel.
Description: First trade paperback edition. | Mechanicsburg, PA : Hellbender Books, 2025.
Summary: Sit in the Devil's Chair at midnight in Cassadaga's Lake Helen Cemetery, and you'll hear sinister whispers by the devil himself. Leave an offering; if it's been interacted with by morning, the devil approves.
Identifiers: ISBN 979-8-88819-393-8 (softcover).
Subjects: FICTION / Horror / Occult & Supernatural | FICTION / Indigenous / Horror | FICTION / Indigenous / Historical.

Designed in the USA
0 1 1 2 3 5 8 13 21 34 55

For the Love of Books!

CONTENTS

FOREWORD

When I approached the Devil's Chair in Cassadaga, Florida, for investigation, I had no preconceived notions. My immediate observation was the remarkable beauty of this unincorporated Volusia County community. Cassadaga exuded a rich cultural atmosphere, evident in the tranquility of Colby Lake and its historic town charm.

As I explored the graveyard and surrounding area of Colby Lake, I encountered an individual who shared their knowledge of the Devil's Chair, immediately capturing my attention. For the purpose of this novel, I have altered names and supplied possible details that were unknown to the person I spoke with.

This is a story based on a legend. If this story inspires you to visit Cassadaga and the chair, always be considerate in your conduct.

Chapter 1

DEVIL'S CHAIR

Present day

Arya ran her hands over the cool stone exterior of the Devil's Chair, half expecting his hand to reach out and grab her. After all, it has been said that this is his chair. Weather-beaten throughout the years, the surface was semi-smooth, and the seat had lost all of its callousness and even had a slight, worn impression in it.

"Take the picture now," Arya said, and grabbed her collar and shook it. "It's hot as shit and I don't want the sweat ruining my makeup. How is my hair?"

"Unchanged," Mila said. "Like it was shaped in the eighties and hasn't moved since."

"Screw you."

"Not today. Sit still and smile. I want you to act like you're sipping a Bahama mama on the deck of a cruise ship."

"Now why would I picture myself on the deck of a cruise ship? Isn't living in Florida supposed to be living in paradise?"

"Well, yeah, I guess so," Mila said. "Until you actually live here. Oh, and here comes the guy that's going to serve you drinks."

"Now you're talking," Arya said, cozying into the seat. "So what does this servant of mine look like?" She cracked a smile.

"He's hot. Well, not just because it's hot out. He's smoking because he's got a nice body that's greased up all nice and shiny. And he's wearing a banana hammock."

1

Arya's shoulders slumped and her smile disappeared. "Seriously, Mila? You had me until the hammock thingy." She pretended to vomit. "Gross. I was instantly reminded of that time we went to the beach and that old guy with the hairy chest—"

"Blue."

"What?"

"The hammock he was wearing. It was powder blue."

Arya puffed her cheeks. "Now I ain't kidding. I think I'm going to be sick."

"What wonderful memories we have of living here in paradise." Mila laughed. "Now, on a serious note, I want you to smile and say, blue banana hammock on an old man makes me happy."

Arya gave her the stink eye. She raised her arms and smiled. "How is this?"

"Fabulous!" Mila said and took several pictures.

"I'm getting bitten up," Arya said. "Are you ready to get out of here?"

"I thought you'd never ask." She put her phone away and gathered her things. "And I think we did our due diligence. We have a long ride home and it's starting to get dark."

"Other than the heat, the bugs, the inaction, and the mental picture of the old man, I had a great time," Arya said in a hurry. She started for the path that would take her back to their waiting vehicle.

"Wait. Hang on," Mila said. "Take a few pictures of me! I want to post the visit to our socials. We need to show our seventy-five adoring followers that we both sat in the Devil's Chair and walked away unscathed." Mila smiled. "Well, mostly."

"Yeah, sure, whatever," Arya said, and took the phone from Mila.

Mila got into the chair, crossed her legs and gently smiled, taking her own advice and acting like everything was perfect. Heck, she even pictured a buff twenty-something-year-old guy wearing a banana hammock.

"You've got a shit-eating grin on you right now, and I don't want to know what you're thinking," Arya said, snapped a few pictures, and then swatted at a mosquito. "These damn bugs are tyrants! That freaking thing was buzzing right in my damn ear!"

"One last thing," Mila said and stood. She pulled a bottle of beer out of her pocketbook and placed it on the Devil's Chair.

"Our gift to you. Thank you for having us," Arya said. "Now drink up."

The two girls hurried to the car. Mila got in the driver's seat, and then started the engine and cranked the air conditioning.

"Well, that was underwhelming," Arya said. "And I don't think the experience was worth the bug bites!" She scratched at her forearm. "I hate the way they dive-bomb you!" She shivered. "And their buzzing! They make me want to scream. Why couldn't I find an indoor hobby instead of running through graveyards in one of the hottest states?"

"Because indoor things are boring and I thought the chair was rather cool," Mila said. "It wasn't that bad. I mean, the bugs were beyond horrible. But the chair and the surrounding area are really cool. I get a nostalgic sort of feel."

Arya glared at her. Sweat and frustration coated her face. "Really? Look at me—I'm a hot mess. The humidity is miserable too."

"Hey, you're the one who wanted to come!"

"Well, duh!" Arya adjusted the air vents on the car's dashboard so the cold air was right in her face. Her hair still hadn't moved. "After that night at the Devil Tree, it only made sense to come to this place next."

"The Devil Tree and the Devil's Chair—I'm noticing the themes. Welcome to Florida, people. Maybe we should come back after dark?"

Arya shrugged. "Who knows, maybe it would change the experience?" She sat in silence, mulling the idea. "We can always try it. I felt nothing around the chair. As far as I'm concerned, it's just a cement and brick seat with a bad rap."

"I've always wondered if demons or ghosts or whatever are light sensitive? I mean, why do they wait to come out at night when I can see perfectly fine during the day?"

Arya smiled. "I've wondered that, too. Maybe it has something to do with adding to the creep factor. Ghost code or something. Anyway, let's have a look at those pics before we start the drive home. I'm not having something posted on the internet where I look horrible."

"You're a ghost hunter, not a model on a runway."

"Whatever. Let's have a look."

Mila started flipping through the phone, examining the pictures. "You photograph well, Arya. That says a lot seeing sweat and impatience all over you."

"Ha ha, very funny," she said. "Let me see. I trust you enough, I suppose, but I need to verify."

Mila handed the phone over. She watched Arya zooming in on a picture of herself, and it was obvious she was being vain. "Give it back," she said and went to grab the phone, but Arya was too fast. She pulled the phone away.

"Hang on, I want to see the ones I took of you." Arya scrolled, furrowed her eyebrows, and started to swipe left and right. "That's odd."

"What is?"

"I took multiple pictures of you, but only one of them came out. All the others are black."

"Let me see," Mila said, and looked at the pictures. "Did you have your hand in the way?"

"I don't think so."

"Maybe when you were trying to swat that mosquito?"

Arya shook her head. "No, that was after I took that last picture."

"Are you sure?"

"I think so, yeah."

Mila zoomed in on the one picture that came out correctly. She stared at the screen, her mouth hanging open.

"What is it?"

"Look," Mila said, and handed the phone back to Arya. "What do you see?"

She looked at the phone, then at Mila. "What the hell?"

"That's freaking *really* creepy," Mila said, smiling although nothing about this was funny to her. "Was someone standing behind me while I was sitting there?"

"No, not that I saw at the time. If that were a person, I'm sure I would've noticed them."

"There goes some of our theories. I think we caught a shadow person and we did it during the day."

"I mean, whatever it is, it is clearly there."

Mila's skin goosed. "It's semi-transparent though, right?"

Arya handed her the phone. "Take another look and zoom in over your shoulder. It's right freaking there, standing in the graveyard!"

Mila did, and she could easily see the semi-transparent black figure standing near the fence line by a headstone. "OK, we have to slow down a second here. Remember, cooler heads prevail."

Perhaps it was a trick of light? She wasn't sure, so she referenced the pictures of Arya and looked at that exact spot. The figure was absent from every single picture.

"You have to be shitting me!" Mila said. She shut the car off, then kicked the door open. Arya followed and the two ladies arrived at the chair. Mila held up the phone to compare what was captured versus what she saw with her naked eye.

"Well?"

"Whatever is in this picture isn't there now, and it certainly wasn't in any of the others," Mila said. "Sit back down and let me take another picture. I want to try and recreate it but with you in the seat instead."

Arya shook her head. "I don't want to sit there right now."

"Why?"

"I don't feel good all of a sudden. I want to get out of here and think about everything that's been happening."

"Alright, I understand, but give me another minute," Mila said and moved to the chair and sat. "We need to do this at least. Take my picture. Try to stand in the same spot."

"Mila?" Arya said, her face flushed.

"What is it?"

Arya raised a shaking hand and pointed. "The beer."

Mila looked. In all the confusion, they'd forgotten the now empty beer bottle they left for the devil to drink.

Mila jumped up. "Are you freaking kidding me? Someone has to be messing with us."

"Yeah, like I said, I've had enough. I really want to go," Arya said. And then with a sudden surge of anger, she shouted, "I want to get out of here and now!"

"No, wait! We need to calm down. This is what we came for," Mila said and stood on the bench. She yelled into the graveyard, "You're not scaring us, and you're certainly not going to chase us out of here!"

"Mila, stop and let's just go!"

"No," she said over her shoulder. "I'm not kidding, screw that. We need to try and debunk the things going on here." She turned her attention to the graveyard again. "Did you hear what I said? You're not scaring us!"

As if in response, the empty bottle that was sitting firmly off to the side on the cement chair tipped over and rolled off, falling into the dirt. This prompted the fight-or-flight response in both women, and they ran for the car.

Locking the doors, they started the car, shouting over one another to get out of there as fast as possible. Within seconds, the car sped away.

Chapter ②

EXPECTATIONS

The past

The room was dark, lit by the flickering firelight of a half dozen candles strategically spaced throughout the room. Humidity hung in the air like a heated, sopping wet blanket.

"You need to use your abilities only for good," George said, the sweat on his brow glistening, his tone firm but not offensive.

Clyde sighed, his eyes fluttering with his frustration. He left home so he wouldn't be spoken down to or lectured ever again. What was the use in trying to start over if this is the way things would always be?

"Do good," George reiterated, slapping Clyde's knee. "It's a very simple rule. I want you to understand that I haven't seen someone so young with such honed skills. What you have is a gift and it needs to be treated with care."

George paused the conversation to light more candles. The thumping of each footfall on the wooden planks sounded like a beating drum, building the tension. The dancing firelight cast eerie shadows on the ceiling, walls, and floor of the small, single-level shack that looked like it couldn't stand up to a stiff wind. Although it was only a temporary living situation, it was still concerning that they were in Florida, where nature seemed most unpredictable and violent.

"I sure do appreciate your compliments and guidance, Mr. Colby," Clyde said. "I hear what you're saying."

"You hear, but I want to make sure you're listening," George said as he waved a finger in the air to emphasize his point. "I cannot have someone in my school with nefarious intent."

Clyde nodded.

"You do understand that, don't you?"

Clyde furrowed his brow. He thought he already answered that. And what kind of question was that anyway? He wasn't stupid and worked hard to keep the bite out of his voice. "Yes, of course I do."

"That's good to hear," George said and sat. He turned away and coughed, deep and hacking. He patted his chest. "Excuse me."

"Are you OK?"

"Yes, thank you. It's just a minor irritation."

"That didn't sound minor, Mr. Colby."

"I'll be fine. Now, I want you to know that this is an open dialogue between you and me. I want to know if there is anything on your mind? Anything you might want to talk about in private with me?"

Clyde shifted uncomfortably and then shrugged. "I'm not sure what you mean?"

"I'm looking to get to know you on a more personal level, Clyde. Perhaps there is something you need to get off your chest. Or maybe there's something you'd like to discuss that you have a hard time talking about with others?"

Clyde leaned forward and rested his elbows on his knees, folding within thoughts about himself. He searched within, struggling to come up with something.

"Maybe it's an event from your past that you or someone would want to know about you. Perhaps some depth to the reasons you left?"

"Arizona," Clyde said.

"Yes, that's right, Arizona. That's a long way away."

"Yes it is, Mr. Colby." Clyde sat upright. "I'm really trying hard to make conversation with your line of questioning, but there is nothing more than what I've already told you."

"Very well," George said.

"I'm really confused right now, Mr. Colby. Do I seem like someone harboring secrets? That I'm hiding something significant from you?"

George took a moment. "I feel as though you're distracted by something. The spirits are trying to tell me something, and, for the first time in as long as I can remember, I can't hear what they're trying to tell me."

"Is that bad?" Clyde said.

"I suppose that is what I was trying to find out by asking you here, to my living quarters, so we could talk. I was hoping to gain more insight and understanding."

"I don't understand." He shifted uncomfortably in his seat. "Your guides have made you think I'm keeping a nefarious secret?"

George shrugged. "They do their best to communicate with me. Having done this for as long as I have, the things I've learned about people hardly ever lead me to surprise. Everyone has something they'd prefer others didn't know."

"I'm almost sorry to disappoint you."

"Well, no need for us to run in circles," George said. "I am satisfied with our interactions. I hope to see you in class tomorrow?"

Clyde stood, extended a hand, and said, "Of course you will see me tomorrow. I'll be here as long as you'll have me."

George met his hand and placed his other hand over the grasp. Clyde immediately identified the tactic he was using—psychometry. It was mainly used to gain information through physical contact.

George gave Clyde's hand a firm squeeze, and let go after a few moments. "Tomorrow it is then. Thank you for your time, Clyde." He walked Clyde to the door and closed it after he left.

George watched Clyde until he disappeared out of sight. Retiring from observing his newest pupil with a sigh, he grabbed a candle and went to his desk, pulled out his ledger, and wrote down some thoughts he had on his continued interaction and spiritual growth concerning Clyde.

When he put ink to paper, no words came to mind. Frustrated and uncertain, he knew he had to take a different approach. He needed to be careful in the selection process. Not everyone who came would be a good fit for the spiritual camp. A good candidate needed to be open and trustworthy.

The main problem was that everyone around him was still in the beginning stages of their spiritual development, and uncertainty was part of their evolution. This, in most instances, was likely because the relationship between the sensitive and their guide was in its infancy or unestablished. Simply put, it was like the plug to a lamp not pushed into the socket all the way. And George needed to remind himself that no matter how far ahead Clyde seemed to be, he was still unrefined.

He pursed his lips as his mind flipped through the faces that surrounded him during the day. Not only was it his responsibility to help them grow spiritually, it was also his responsibility to keep them safe. The last thing he wanted to do was put someone in harm's way. That included both their physical and mental well-being. The early phases were the most influential and delicate.

It was time to retire for the night and there would be plenty of time during class tomorrow to choose and recruit his ally. That relationship would be significant. He could use them to help understand others. No. Use was not the correct word. *Leverage.* That was what he would do.

And as much as he hated to admit it, that relationship would be used especially for Clyde. Trying to read his character had proven not only to be difficult, but physically and mentally exhausting, too.

Chapter ③

EVIDENCE

Present day

Arya answered the door to find Mila standing there with two coffees in hand. There was a bag at her feet, and a bright smile showed her teeth.

"I come bearing gifts!"

"You're a savior!" Arya said and held the door for Mila.

"How did you sleep?"

Arya grabbed the bag and brought it inside. "Hardly. You?"

"Yeah, much of the same," Mila said and handed Arya her coffee. "Light and sweet. Just the way you like it."

Arya held up the coffee. "If you hadn't brought me this, I would've been back in bed already trying to make up for the sleep I've lost."

"I was always told that you can't make up for lost sleep. Lost sleep is just lost sleep."

"Yeah, yeah," Arya said, rolling her eyes. "You don't have to always be so specific. People speak in generalities sometimes."

"Yeah, like the weatherman. Chance of rain. Annoying."

"Don't be this irritating so early." Arya took a sip of coffee. "And just because you say so doesn't mean I'm not going to try and catch up on lost sleep and that it's not worth the effort. Don't judge."

"Well someone woke up on the wrong side of the bed."

Arya growled.

"So what did you think of yesterday?" Mila asked.

"Which part?"

11

Mila took a seat at the table. "The entire thing, I guess. Now that we've had a little time to think about it, maybe things are a bit clearer."

"It was all a little unbelievable, I suppose. Everything happened so fast it was really hard to absorb what was going on. I guess I'm puzzled? God only knows what we actually missed in all of that confusion."

"Yeah, there was a lot going on for sure." Mila pointed at the bag she brought. "Can you hand me that?"

Arya picked up the bag and set it in front of Mila. She sat next to her. "Do I dare ask what's in there?"

"Ask and you shall receive. What say you?"

"OK, I'll bite. What's in the bag?"

"Man, am I glad you asked," Mila said with a smile and started rummaging through the contents. "Like you, I was tossing and turning all night. The empty beer, the shadow figure, the thick atmosphere that gave us quite the fright . . . It was all a bit much. Overwhelmed is the best way I can describe how I felt."

"Tell me about it. I was really on edge, and I think I still am."

"We both were, and I'm absolutely convinced that what we experienced was far more than a jump-scare event. With that said, I decided I would get up early and head out and be productive. I did something I thought might help us understand. So I figured, what the hell, it's not like I could sleep anyways. My mind has been running like crazy since, and I can't seem to locate the off switch."

Arya waved her arms. "I know you and your big ideas. I am not doing a Ouija. No freaking way."

Mila laughed. "It's not a Ouija, but you're a wuss."

"I was tempted to do it once but thought better of it. And thank god I left it alone. Inviting that crap into my life willingly probably would've sent me over the edge."

"I don't want you going back there," Mila said, and tapped her temple. "I'm glad things are improving for you. With that said, respectfully, I'm going to pivot. Let's stay in the present."

Arya nodded. "Thank you for that. Yesterday was so intense, and I know this sounds crazy, but I could literally feel the energy. It was like we were standing in a vortex. The hair on my arms was standing."

"I understand what you're saying because mine were, too. The atmosphere was charged," Mila said, and withdrew a thickly folded paper out of the bag. "It was like an invisible lightning storm all around us. We're lucky one of us didn't get turned into the Flash." She took her time to open it. "So I went to the UPS store and had a poster made."

"A poster?"

"Yeah, like an actual poster." She opened the poster completely and placed it flat on the table. Mila turned it so Arya could see it at the proper angle. She watched her friend's expression go from curiosity to surprise and eventually to dread.

"You've got to be kidding me!" Arya said, covering her mouth.

"That's what I thought, too. I think seeing it like this makes it more real somehow."

"Yeah, it does," Arya said, and she showed Mila the goosed flesh on her arms.

As plain as day, the poster was a duplicate of the exact picture that had captured the black mass at the Devil's Chair yesterday. It looked like a person standing off in the distance behind Mila. Now that it was bigger and seemingly yanked forward to something more life-sized, it was even more authentic and creepy. The head, arms, and body, draped in either a dress or cloak, were easy to see and undeniable. And yet, the apparition was semi-transparent.

"I think it's looking at you," Mila said. "I mean, look at the way the head is tilted seemingly right past me and to you."

"I don't think there's any denying that," Arya said as she shivered. "That thing looking at me doesn't feel good. It's creepy as hell."

"I don't have an explanation as to what that is. Is it a person? A demon? Or maybe there is a simpler answer, like a camera glitch."

"Perhaps there is. For a lot of reasons, I hope so."

"And we both know we need to go back there for that very reason and try to debunk it."

"I agree."

"You do?"

"Yeah, why?"

"You know, because of the things you told me and the thing I'm trying to help you avoid. Sometimes I think we shouldn't dabble because of that."

"Well, I appreciate that, but I can't just shut my curiosity off."

"I don't think you should." She sighed. "I sound like a politician. You should and then you shouldn't. What I'm trying to say is that I thought you were going to be too freaked out or whatever and that I would have to convince you. Even though I shouldn't."

"You're a bigger mess than me. And I know that's why you brought me the damn coffee." Arya shook her head and raised a brow. "Quite cunning if you ask me."

"And the reason I had that poster made," Mila said. "I figured it would either scare us away or make us want to go back."

"I can't let this be what we've come away with and not go any further. Like I said, I can't just shut it off. That's like writing a sentence and purposely not putting a period at the end."

Mila shivered. "Wow, could you use a more annoying metaphor? And yeah, even though it's really freaky, I agree that it can't be left like that."

"Whatever that is, it's unfinished."

The girls stood in silence, their focus on the poster and the image of the apparition.

"So?" Arya said, but the word came out more like a sigh.

"So . . . when do you think we should do this?"

Arya took a second and drummed her fingers on the tabletop. "I'm not going to lie." She pointed at the giant poster and settled her finger on the face of the apparition and, ultimately, the hollow-looking eyes. "This thing that seems to be looking at me." She tapped the picture with a stiff finger. "We don't know if it's good or bad or what it even wants. We know it takes a hell of a lot of energy for an apparition to manifest. At the very least, that means it wanted us to see it."

Mila nodded. "It is possible it showed itself so it could draw us back."

"Yeah, and a big part of me believes that's exactly what it was doing. And if that's what its intent was, it worked. That shows intelligence, and we need to investigate this location with caution."

"Investigators investigating the thing that wants to be investigated. Sounds rad."

"And you're a nerd."

"Any concerns about our safety?"

Arya folded her arms. "Now that was the most obvious fishing expedition ever. Go on, get it out. What are you getting at?"

"Devon."

"Sure, OK. What about him?"

"Well, I sent him a copy of the picture of our friend here last night, and he said he would come with us. Of course, he said he'll bring some equipment to help capture more evidence. That was the whole reason I contacted him about this anyway."

"That's fantastic."

"So that's it? It's fantastic? You're not mad at me?"

"What's the point? It's done. You'll blame it on your lack of sleep and never the fact that you've had a crush on him for as long as I can remember."

"Arya?"

"It's OK, Mila, really. I know he's your boyfriend and that it had to be done sooner or later. The later has become the sooner."

Mila studied Arya, unsure.

"Seriously, Mila, it's OK." The girls stared at each other for a long while before Arya said, "What else?"

"I spent some time last night doing in-depth research on the Devil's Chair and things that may be important to what might be going on there. Of course, in my ever-increasing thoroughness, I've included the surrounding area as well."

"And? What did you dig up?"

"A lot of interesting stuff actually. There is a spiritualist camp not too far from the Devil's Chair, founded in the 1800s by a man named George Colby." Mila referenced notes that she took on her phone. "He was born in 1848 and was baptized in 1860. This event seemed to be the catalyst that awakened his spiritualistic knowledge. Later in life, he was actually known for his healing and psychic abilities."

"Interesting."

"Yes it is, but I think it gets even better."

"I don't know how that's possible."

"Hear me out. George Colby was told he would one day find a spiritualist camp in the southern portion of the United States."

"Told by who?"

"His guide."

"No way."

"Way."

"Alright, you weren't kidding," Arya said, rubbing her hands. "This is getting good."

"Soon after his awakening, he acquired a set of spirit-guides. One was supposedly a very powerful Native American who called himself Seneca."

"Seneca. That sounds like a soda. By the way, what is a spiritualist camp?"

"From what I gathered, it's a place where people learn to hone their abilities; to become more connected to the spiritual universe around them and learn how to form and cultivate that relationship."

Arya stared at Mila. "Hold on a second and back up a bit. What type of abilities are we talking about?"

"Psychic gifts," Mila said. "Pineal gland coming online? A near-death experience that had them returning with more than they left with? I don't really understand any of this or what triggers it. There are a whole bunch of theories, but nothing definitive. Some people doubt its existence completely, calling it nothing but parlor tricks and blah blah blah. But we know psychics are real. That aside, and get this, the camp is still freaking active. I mean, like, active even today!"

"A lot of the things you're saying have my attention on a personal level," Arya said as she heaved a sigh. "Listen, Mila, the last thing I want to do is piss people off by invading their space. Especially psychics."

"Ah, Arya." She waved a hand at her and rolled her eyes. "Voodoo scares me, psychics don't. And right now, we're just asking questions about an experience we both shared. Innocent stuff. The picture and the beer are a lot to happen in such a short amount of time. Don't forget how we were reacting with fear, anger, and fight or flight. That is a lot of activity and an unordinary reaction that this shadow person pulled out of us. Especially for only one visit and to do it in such a short time period."

"I don't disagree with any of that." Arya took a sip of her coffee. "If I know you, I'd have to say that these things we're talking about are the reasons you decided to call Devon. You were just looking for an excuse."

"Maybe, maybe not. There's a lot going on there, and we can really use his help."

"I don't want it to be just him and me," Arya said. "I don't know how we're going to be, and I guess I want you there just in case things go bad."

"I'll be there for you," Mila said, and nodded her understanding. "I wouldn't do that unless you told me it was OK to do that."

"I know you wouldn't, but I just needed to say it," Arya said. "That whole best friend thing might complicate things for you. Sometimes I feel like you've been between us forever."

Mila shook her head. "It's not complicated for me at all. We've always said sisters before misters. Well, that, and best friends no matter what." Mila held her coffee up for Arya to cheers. They tapped cups and drank to it.

"OK, what else did you unearth?" Arya asked.

"To drill down a bit deeper into some of the details about that place, it is said that the area has the highest concentration of sensitives. We're talking higher than any other place in the world."

"That's intense. No wonder the place is so active and the air seemed to literally crackle with energy when the activity started."

"Yeah. I suppose with all of that energy around, the spirits have an endless food source."

"That, and all the people that go there to see the infamous chair probably create another energy source. Ya got anything else?"

"I guess we'll find out. I'll message Devon and I'll tell him you're cool with everything. I'll see when and what time he wants us to pick him up and organize everything for us to head back out to the chair."

chapter 4

FULL OF GRACE

The past

"Can I offer you anything to eat or drink?" George asked as he placed a lit candle at the center of a side table. Two wingback chairs were placed on either side of the table facing an unlit, dilapidated fireplace. Even at this time of night, it was far too hot and humid for a fire.

"No, but thank you," Grace said from one of the chairs. Her voice quivered. "I ate something and freshened up after school."

"I want you to know that I appreciate you coming over here on such short notice," George said as he sat in the chair next to Grace. "I would like for this meeting to be confidential. Can I count on that?"

"Of course," Grace said. "If I'm to be honest, I'm a little nervous about my being here, in your home. I feel like I'm in the principal's office and I don't know what I did. I hope I didn't do anything wrong or that I'm not operating to your standards."

"Quite the opposite," George said, giving her a gentle smile. "And this here"—he motioned to her and then to himself—"this is nothing more than an innocent conversation." He pressed his back into the chair and crossed his legs. He ran his hand over his Hungarian-style mustache and twirled the ends with his fingers as he fell into private thoughts. "Aside from what we've already talked about, I am looking for your insight and, of course, above all, your honesty in the matters I want to further discuss and explore."

"OK," Grace said. She sat upright, stiff and sweating. This wasn't a normal occurrence to be invited into George Colby's living quarters, and her pounding heart verified that. Was this some sort of test? If it were, she was certain she would pass with flying colors. She was serious about her spiritual growth. Because of these gifts, she lost all the people in her life. They thought something was wrong with her, and some were emphatic that she was possessed. Once that accusation came out, it spread like wildfire and she was forced to flee for fear of her personal safety. But she was here now, sitting with the one man that could help her fully understand her gifts and learn how to control them. It was her hope to one day help others in situations similar to her own. So she exhaled with a huff and tried to will the tremble out of her hands.

"Relax, Grace. Your participation and growth in our cause are nothing short of impressive. I'm not ashamed to say I need you as much as you seem to think you need me."

"Thank you," Grace said, and felt her body sink into the chair. The compliment allowed a much-needed release of the tension, and she smiled. Then her shoulders fell forward and she stifled a nervous laugh. "I really appreciate your saying so, Mr. Colby. That means so much coming from you."

George met Grace with a smile of his own. "And your saying that means a lot to me as well. I hope you see we're not that much different from each other. Now that we've got the pleasantries out of the way, I'd like to ask if you have an opinion, or perhaps, a reading on Clyde Stolly?"

"Clyde Stolly?" Grace said as her gaze moved around the room as if the answer she and George were seeking were there somewhere, floating around, waiting to be seen.

George nodded, his expression not giving any direction in which she should go. It became obvious that this interaction needed to be natural.

Grace leaned her head back and closed her eyes. "I can try and do a reading." She concentrated on her breathing and searched her mind and feelings. Almost immediately she could feel the answer George sought was there, but just out of reach. She moved her attention deeper into the void, looking to unveil that which wished to remain hidden.

"I've found you," Grace whispered, the moment a major breakthrough. Never had she been able to channel with such speed and clarity.

"What do you see?" George said, his voice restrained.

Grace squeezed her eyes shut and tried to pierce the black. "I don't know. Whatever it is, it's trying to hide from me. It's elusive, but I can hear it laughing. Whatever it is, it sounds maniacal." She continued to inspect her vision, hesitating with necessary caution. "No, I don't think I have that right. I'm feeling something is . . . playful?"

"Don't retract," George coached. "Stay there for a moment. If you don't pursue it, it may come to you. If it's something manifested from evil or, as you were suggesting, is playful, it may want to show itself. I suggest you don't press. It is my experience that they don't like to be ignored. After all, what is the fun in that?"

"I do. I see a child." She pursed her lips and shook her head. "I can't see his face. He's sitting on the floor playing jackstraw by himself and he doesn't notice me."

"I may have been wrong. I want you to be careful, but can you get closer so that you might get a look at his face?"

"I think so." Grace nodded and licked her lips. She moved forward, but instead of physical steps, she drifted. Once she got beside the boy, she bent over and reached a cautious hand out in an attempt to pull the obscurity away. It was thin, but hanging there, in the way.

"Hello?" she said, and oddly, the child continued to play as if he were completely oblivious to her presence. Just as her hand touched the veil of division, she was yanked from her spell by an abrupt sound.

Thump! Thump! Thump!

Grace gasped and George's attention shifted to the door. He held a finger to his lips, asking Grace for quiet. Grace's eyes were wide, her breathing fast, but she wasn't making noise.

George opened the door less than a foot.

"Clyde?" he said, finding it impossible to hide his surprise.

"Mr. Colby. I'd like to continue our conversation from last night. My mind has been troubled, and I've had some time to think your questions through. I wanted to discuss some things with you, if that is OK?"

George took a small step forward, his one hand controlling the door as he pulled it tight against his body, preventing Clyde from getting a look inside. "Now is not a good time. Perhaps tomorrow night?"

"I'm sorry, I didn't mean to interrupt. Do you have a guest?"

"No," he said, but he didn't know why he had lied. Who was there and whatever the reason was, wasn't Clyde's business. Either way, it didn't matter. George said what he said and needed to move on, and if that meant moving around those words, then that's what he would do. "But I am busy with work and have to get back to it."

"I'm sure your hands are full with your plans for building the community." Clyde bowed his head. "I'm sorry. I don't know why I didn't think of that."

"Thank you for your consideration and for your understanding."

He looked at George with wide, expecting eyes. "Please keep in mind that I could be of assistance to you as you move closer to construction. I have a lot of experience and have a firm understanding of carpentry."

George smiled. "I may take you up on that offer once we get to that stage. I can always use a good pair of hands."

Clyde shifted, and it was obvious to George that he was trying to scan as much of the inside of the house as he could. In that instant, he wished he hadn't lied. That was stupid.

"OK, Mr. Colby. I guess I'll be on my way then."

"Call me George, please. Shall we get together tomorrow night?" George turned away and gave in to the tickle sensation in his chest. A whooping cough shook his body.

"I hate to say it, but that sounds like it is getting worse," Clyde said. "Are you sure you're OK?"

"I'm OK, and I do appreciate your concern." He looked into the house for effect, rubbed his chest, and then looked back at Clyde. "Alright, I've gotta get back to work. Remember tomorrow night."

"Yes, absolutely! Tomorrow night it is then," Clyde said. "I guess that'll allow me enough time to arrange my thoughts a little bit better. I hope my showing up here didn't seem hasteful or intrusive. I don't want to send the wrong message."

"Think nothing of it. I'm looking forward to our meeting," George said and closed the door. He moved to the window and watched Clyde walking away. "Do you think his timing is a bit odd?"

"I thought that while listening to your conversation," Grace said. "It felt forced and a bit clumsy. You don't think he's been listening by the windows, do you?"

George looked at the windows and their coverings. He inspected them. "No, I don't think so," he said, uncertain. Stepping back and looking at the windows, he couldn't see out, but knew when the candles were lit on the inside of the dwelling at night, things inside were much easier to see from the outside.

The construction of his dwelling was merely temporary until his plans were finalized and the permanent housing could be erected. Thus leaving the walls a bit thinner, the structure feeble, his privacy vulnerable. Upon Grace's mention, now the idea of sound carrying was a cause for concern.

"I'll be right back," George said, then went outside and shut the door so he could look at the windows from the perspective Clyde had. The flickering candlelight and the dimness of the interior made it almost impossible to make out any detail. The voices, on the other hand, that could or could not have been heard through the walls would have to be tested. Most likely, if Clyde heard them, it might come out in his inquiry to understand. And, if Clyde hadn't really departed, it would look odd if he were to call out to Grace and test how the sound carried right now.

"I don't think he could see within," George said when he came back in and closed the door. "The candlelight is dim, and I couldn't make out where you were."

"That's good," Grace said, then stood. "If you don't mind, can we continue this tomorrow?"

"Absolutely, Grace," George said. "Are you feeling OK?"

"I'm finding myself to be a bit tired from my interaction with the child."

"Your skills and the information you provided are impressive, Grace," George said, offering her a hand. She took it, and he assisted her to her feet.

"Thank you."

"Your guide? Have you made that connection yet?"

Grace huffed. "No." She shook her head. "Like what just happened, I see things. Like I'm being shown. There is no dialogue and it can be hard for me to interpret. I don't know what she looks like, and I find that to be so frustrating."

"You did wonderfully tonight. I believe that time will reveal more details of what you were seeing. I'm certain of it. Your fatigue will go away as you learn to hone your skills and protect your energy. It takes time, practice, and patience. Perhaps we should get together before the camp meeting to go over some techniques? We could continue to try and establish that connection."

"That would be wonderful. I can be here an hour before, if that works for you?"

"It does," George said. "May I walk you to your quarters?"

Grace waved a dismissive hand. "That won't be necessary, Mr. Colby."

"Please, like I said to Clyde, call me George," he said, and walked her to the door.

Chapter 5

VANDALS

Present day

Arya and Mila stood in front of a small, unremarkable, weather-beaten gravestone that read:

GEO. P. COLBY
JAN 6, 1848
JULY 27, 1933

"So this is where he was buried?"

"It certainly appears that way."

"Jeez," Arya said, mindlessly moving a spotty patch of grass blades with her foot. "This definitely is not what I was expecting. All of a sudden, I have an overwhelming feeling of being sad." She fought back tears. "God, I feel like I have to cry."

"Me too," Mila said, then stepped away and fanned herself with her hand. "It's really sad. I don't know if it was because we were searching for his grave and I was expecting something so much more, or maybe it was your reaction." Tears fell from her eyes and she wiped them away. "I mean, it seems like he was bigger than life in all that he influenced and created." She opened her arms. "Look at the area. His thumbprint is everywhere you look."

"Yeah," Arya said. "It's really sad. No matter what we were in life, we all end up here, in some box with dirt thrown on top of us." She raised her voice. "But don't worry, we get an engraving on a rock no bigger than a damn shoebox." She paused, trying to organize her thoughts. "Hopefully there is something beyond this shitty world."

"Now I'm thoroughly depressed." Mila sighed, her eyes red from crying. "It's really weird how things have led up to us being here, in front of George's grave. The idea to visit the chair, the apparition, and our need to know more. It's almost foreboding. I can't pretend I understand how spiritual warfare even works, if that is what this is. But something is pulling the levers, and we're moving around like we're their pawns."

Arya's shoulders slumped forward. "It sure seems that way, doesn't it?"

Silence inserted itself as the girls contemplated the idea of a concentration being orchestrated by something they couldn't hear or see.

"Damn," Mila said. "This is such a heavy feeling, and it happened right when we found his headstone."

"I was going to say that, too," Arya said, distant. Over the past few days, they were in the midst of poltergeist activity, apparitions and a push and pull of energy that was so strong, they could feel it. She shivered and snapped to, and said, "We need to shake the blues and stay focused. Can you show me the photo of the apparition?"

Mila took out her phone and quickly accessed the photo. The girls studied it. Just like the other day when they went to debunk the image, there was nothing they could see that would create the illusion of what appeared in the photo.

"Are you thinking what I'm thinking?"

Arya shrugged. "I don't know what I'm thinking half the time, let alone what you might be thinking."

"Follow me," Mila said.

They walked to the location where the apparition had manifested itself. Again, there wasn't anything obvious that could create such a disparity from one picture to the next. In the first series of pictures with Arya sitting on the chair, there was nothing out of the ordinary in the background. And then the shadow seemingly appeared, only to have the camera take photographs that were completely black.

"I'm convinced we caught someone in that picture that was probably a living person at one time. Taking that into consideration, we both agree it wanted to be seen. Whatever is happening here, it is something that exists outside of our understanding. I was thinking we could look at the headstones over here. Maybe we can look up the names and see if anything comes up."

"That's a great idea," Arya said. "Because whoever that is has made a great effort in making themselves known. I have no doubt they wanted us to see them, and they wanted us to come back here. Maybe the theory of them using energy is the way they can communicate? Perhaps they wanted us to come back so they could use our energy to guide us and place us here. They have something to tell us."

"And here we stand, offering ourselves," Mila said. "There aren't any headstones over here."

"It was a good theory. So what do you think it is trying to say to us?"

Mila took a moment to ponder the question. "I wish the answer was written down and handed to us."

"Wouldn't that be nice?"

"It would certainly make things much easier for us. But we know that won't happen. So it looks like we have a mystery to solve."

The girls sank into silence, their eyes sweeping throughout the grave-yard and the surrounding area. It was possible the image of the shadow person had a reasonable and traditional explanation, and if it did, it wasn't standing out, pushing them to believe it was supernatural.

"Why do people do this?" Arya asked with a bite to her tone. The frustration took hold and began to manifest in her words and actions. She stomped her foot.

The graveyard had been subjected to vandals who had no respect for the dead, no respect for property, and with that, zero respect for the memory of these people and their loved ones who still came to visit.

Mila shook her head. "I was thinking the same thing. I don't know why, but clearly, we can agree that it's senseless. And for what reason would someone need to desecrate headstones? It's a meaningless act carried out only to hurt and defile."

"I don't think we'll ever know the reasons why because we don't think like that. Behavior like that doesn't register in our brains."

"The world is a beautiful place. As soon as you put people in it, everything gets screwed up."

"Amen to that. And I'm sorry," Arya said. "I'm upsetting you, too."

"Don't be. You . . . they have the right to be upset."

"They are affecting our moods."

"I noticed it started the moment we found his headstone."

"I take that as a sign that we're on the right path. We need to be mindful and careful of that."

"I read that the community guards the graveyard," Mila said. "I know this to be especially true during Halloween because it brings out people looking for a thrill. And by the looks of things, that brings out the worst in people. Mob mentality is one of the lowest forms of societal destructive behaviors."

"Let's be blunt: They think it's a pass to act like an asshole."

"I couldn't have said it any better myself. I think everyone should behave like their momma's are always watching them."

"Yeah, they should." Arya kicked a rock that tumbled a few feet away. "The veil between the living and the dead is supposed to be thinnest during Halloween."

Mila lowered her voice to a whisper. "Even though we can't see anyone, we're probably being watched right now."

"By, like, people?"

"Yes. And who knows, probably other things, too?"

"That's a creepy thought but most likely true," Arya said. "If people only knew what was making things go bump in the night, a lot of them would never go looking for them."

"Well, the things you told me really opened my eyes and got me interested in doing this."

"I'm glad I could turn some of those experiences into something positive." Arya stuffed her hands into her pockets. "And who knows? Maybe the spirits stand around talking like us, trying to figure out what to do next."

"Well, if that's true, we could use a little help. So if you're listening, please tell us what to do next."

They both paused and listened. When no response came forth, Arya said, "I think we should go back to the chair and recreate what we did and see what kind of response we get. Then, when we come back with Devon tomorrow, we should have a better idea where to start."

"I think that's a great idea."

The girls walked together, and Mila settled into the Devil's Chair while Arya prepared her cell phone.

"Did you bring a beer for when we leave?"

Arya patted her pocketbook. "Got it."

"How about we take a few-minute video before we snap some stills to get the lay of the land?"

"Sure," Arya said, preparing her phone. "How did anyone live without these things?"

"I know, right?" Mila nodded toward the graveyard. "Of course I mean no offense to them."

Arya looked at the graveyard and said, "I don't think they mind. By the way, how does my hair look?"

"Unmoved as usual," Mila said.

"You know I've got to be ready for camera time," she said. She held her phone up, an arm's distance away, and began recording herself. "This is Arya." She spun and got Mila in the background. "And I'm here with my bestie, Mila. We're at the Devil's Chair in Cassadaga, Florida, investigating the strange."

Mila stood and positioned herself right behind Arya. She tilted her head, smiled, and held up two fingers.

Arya continued, "It is said that you can hear the devil whispering in your ear if you sit alone in his chair at the stroke of midnight. That if you leave a closed beer behind, the devil will drink it without ever opening it. As outlandish as these claims are, we felt they deserved some attention. We just started investigating this location, and we wanted to let you know we're going to share our findings with you. I don't want to tease, but it has already delivered in a big way.

"Even though the Devil's Chair is located inside an allegedly haunted cemetery, it's beautiful and even peaceful here. Unfortunately, the cemetery shows signs of being desecrated by vandals. If you're going to come here, we ask you to respect the land and the people that were put to rest here."

Mila nodded in agreement. "You can come here. Anyone and everyone! But we can enjoy this place and the legend and intrigue without trying to screw stuff up!"

Arya stopped the recording. "Spontaneous, but I think that was pretty good. I like the way you went with it."

"You know me, I'm a regular ham." Mila smiled and pointed at her dimples. She got back to business. "I think you're onto something with what you just did. We should do this as an episodic vlog or something. Then we can do a wrap-up video at the end."

Arya nodded. "I like it a lot. The picture of the apparition could be a part of the big reveal, final episode."

"Unless we catch something bigger. If you want, we can film this and approach it by logging our investigation into why the apparition showed itself," Mila said. "We can play into what we already have."

"This is going to be epic and may land us on the paranormal investigator map."

"Things are coming together. Now, let's try and recreate the picture from the other day and see if we catch anything."

"The sun is going down soon, and I brought us something."

"Oh?"

Arya pulled bug spray out of a pack clipped around her waist. Mila's eyes slowly closed and a smile overtook her face. "You are a freaking genius."

Arya tilted her head and held a hand to her ear. "What was that?"

"Shut up," Mila said. "Spray me first and then I'll do you."

Chapter 6

AMBUSH

The past

Grace exited the back door that George held for her. The night air was still and sticky, and the darkness of night was barely interrupted by slivers of moonlight that broke through fast-moving clouds. It was just enough light to keep her from tripping over something and falling flat on her face.

"Thank you, Grace," George said. "Are you sure you don't want me to walk you home?"

"I would prefer you didn't, Mr. Colby. I need to clear my head, and I don't want to risk our secret getting out by people seeing us together. I'll be just fine."

"For the record, I'm uncomfortable not fulfilling my duties by making sure you're home safely. But I know better than to argue with someone who has their mind made up as firmly as you."

"I'll see you in the morning, Mr. Colby—I mean George," Grace said and turned away. The door thumped shut and she walked around the side of the house. She inhaled and had a true appreciation of how beautiful this place would be once George finished with his plans. It was already beautiful, but to imagine the houses built and the spiritualist camp running as its own self-sustained little village excited her. To be a part of it felt like holy fulfillment.

The night breeze gave her a chill. That had to be from her wet skin and exhaustion. Whatever the case, they could all use a reprieve from the stifling, unrelenting heat that left their skin sticky and energy levels low. Sometimes it was impossible to get anything done during the day, and because of the constant sweat, all it seemed like she did was drink, pee, and bathe.

"Hmm," she said, pausing her walk. The normal ruckus of insects and amphibians trilling, buzzing, and croaking was noticeably absent. "That's strange."

"Grace?"

Grace trembled and turned as she let out a yelp. Her eyes were wide and her own shaking hand covered her mouth.

"I'm sorry," Clyde said. "I didn't mean to scare you."

Her hand went to her heart. "Jesus. What are you doing sneaking up on someone like that?"

"I wasn't sneaking. I saw you and wanted to talk." Clyde pointed at Grace's dwelling that was off in the distance. "I stopped by your place, but you didn't answer and I didn't see any candlelight. I've been working through some thoughts and was taking in some night air before I was going to return home."

"Hang on a second here, Clyde. Were you purposely waiting around for me to come back home?"

Clyde sneezed. "Excuse me?"

"Bless you."

"Thank you," he said and looked around for a long moment. "But I was asking you to excuse me for your accusation that I am somehow stalking you, not for my sneezing. I like to be polite, but you seem awfully defensive and are directing aggression toward me for no good reason. I can't help but wonder why? Where were you? What are you trying to hide?"

Grace reeled. "How dare you!"

"Your tone reflects exactly how I feel. So really, if you're going to be the first to cast a stone, why don't you entertain me? Tell me where you were."

"I don't think that's really any of your business." Grace motioned to walk away and Clyde grabbed her arm.

"Don't touch me," she said, spinning to face him before she pulled away.

Clyde let her go and stepped back. "Grace, I just want to talk. I'm sorry I scared you. I really am. I know things are coming off a bit weird right now, but that's not my intention, as I'm sure it isn't yours."

Grace took a step back. "Your people skills leave a lot to be desired. If you're looking to win people over, I don't think you're going about it the right way. When you frighten someone, especially a lady, by coming out of nowhere, instead of apologizing, you jump to conclusions of a scheme. That makes me question your motive."

"Please forgive me, you're right." Clyde clasped his hands behind his back. "I'm a small-town guy and I'm not as refined as I'd like to be."

"Not even close, sir." Grace stared at him and then broke the tension with a smile. "Now that we've gotten that out of the way, I want to tell you that you really need to work on your manners and that Southwestern accent, too. I'm extending an olive branch and I'm hoping you take it."

Clyde raised his hands in surrender. "I will, and thank you. But I don't know what I can do about the accent."

"You'll figure it out, cowboy. Now I would like to get home. You are more than welcome to walk with me to make sure I get home OK. Of course, I expect you to be a perfect gentleman. Also, don't interrogate me. It's really off-putting."

"I understand. It would be my pleasure to escort you." He stayed in stride with her. "I would like to start over."

"We can talk about this gently, if that's possible, or we shouldn't talk about it at all," Grace said after a long moment of silence. "So let's start with why you want to know where I was?"

"Things feel wrong," Clyde said as he kicked at the small rocks on the path. "A feeling, I guess. My guide is restless but can't explain why. He did tell me he was being watched, but whoever was spying on him disappeared. Me and George had a conversation the night before last about his concern for my direction. What I just told you are the events that transpired since. Yes, I'm on edge, but I feel like something strange is going on, and I don't know why my guide is so confused. Well, what I meant to say was that his and my confusion coupled together has me troubled."

"OK, wow, that was a lot. Is there anything I should be concerned about when it comes to you?"

"Where did that come from?" He scoffed. "You sound exactly like George."

"Well, I am alone and it's nighttime. Although you've always been the perfect gentleman since we met, I'm feeling quite vulnerable right now, so I don't care who you think I sound like."

Clyde nodded and shrugged. "No, when you put it that way, I understand. But I want you to know there's not a harmful bone in my body. I am here to learn and grow like everyone else unless, of course, I'm being naive and there's some greater plan I'm not aware of. I feel like I'm on the outs for some reason. Maybe there's something you can tell me, and if there is, you'd be willing to say it. Is there something I should know or be worrying about?"

"I can't see why you would have anything to worry about if you are being open and honest."

"Of course I am."

"That's a start," Grace said. "Now, why don't you tell me about that conversation you had with Mr. Colby?"

"Well, that feeling I was telling you I had—it is a bad feeling. I don't want to get into the details, but it's like he doesn't trust me or something, and I don't know why. I've somehow gained his suspicion."

"Did he tell you that?"

"Not exactly."

"So what's the problem?"

"I stopped by his house a little while ago because I wanted to talk to him." Clyde stopped walking. "He sent me away as if he were trying to hide something from me."

Grace stood with him. "I'm not following."

"He told me he had work to do, that he was alone."

Grace could feel her cheeks redden.

"I know you were there. I heard you. The thing is, I don't know why he lied to me and why you are, too." He looked away. "It's really disappointing."

"I'm sorry to hear that. But I think that's something you are going to have to take up with him. You can't expect me to get between the two of you."

"No," Clyde said. "I don't suppose that would be reasonable."

Grace began to walk again and she quickened her pace. Her living quarters were close and that meant the end of this conversation, too. "But my going to him tonight has absolutely nothing to do with you. You're not the only member of this community, and certainly you're not the only member that deserves George's attention or the expected privacy of those talks."

"Hmm," Clyde responded, barely loud enough for Grace to hear. He put his hands on his hips and heaved a sigh.

"So no matter what I say to you, you won't believe me. And because of that, I feel the need to ask you, what's the point of this conversation? Should I be feeling bad, too, about the way you're doubting me?"

Clyde stopped ten feet shy of her door. "Do you have a spirit-guide, Grace?"

She kept walking. "You know I do. Everyone here does. Why?"

"Do you trust them?"

"I haven't met her yet, but of course I do. She's my guide. Trust means everything."

"For me too," Clyde said, and turned his face to the wind. "But I don't think you want to know what mine is saying about you right now."

Chapter ⑦

NIGHTFALL

Present day

Arya, Mila, and Devon arrived at the Devil's Chair. Night had fallen and the streets had been quiet for several hours. They parked the car two blocks away and walked to the cemetery, getting the lay of the land while they did so. Conversation between them was kept to a minimum as they purposely looked and made sure they weren't being watched.

Using the cover of darkness and ignoring the signs that informed visitors that the cemetery closed at dusk, the group used the outer perimeter of the large graveyard, cordoned off by a chain-link fence, to sneak to the Devil's Chair.

"It feels much different at night," Arya said.

Mila shivered. "Yes. Much. It's heavier."

"We were here yesterday to try and gather more information on what we captured on film," Arya said to Devon. "We both had a mood change, but this place, right now, feels like it had the mood change. It feels dark."

"How about you, Devon? Are you feeling anything?" Mila asked.

"I hadn't even heard of this place before. And yeah, I can tell you that the air is thick. Heavy. It's really a weird feeling," Devon said. He spun where he stood, looking around. "I don't know why, but I feel like we're being watched."

The girls exchanged a look but didn't say anything. The consistency couldn't be ignored.

"It's odd. I haven't experienced anything quite like this before," he said. "I mean, it literally feels like we're being watched." The cumbersome

35

duffel bag slung over his shoulder swung with his movement. It was packed with ghost-hunting equipment they had used many times before and were prolific with. "Look at this."

Devon held out his arm. Goosebumps and raised hair showed his physical reaction to the environment they were in.

"I feel it, too," Arya said. She held out her arm, which revealed the exact same thing. "I'm getting the same reaction, and Mila and I have experienced that before. You having that happen almost immediately upon arrival is validation that our bodies are reacting to something here."

"But what?" Mila said.

"Well, if we're going to figure that out, we need to get right into this," Devon said. "We need to document while the opportunity is presenting itself. I don't want us missing anything. I'm going to start the digital recorder."

"Maybe we should replicate your being in the chair when we caught that evidence," Arya said to Mila. "I'll be in the same area. I'm going to put the trigger object out, so when you're ready to start asking questions, just get into it." Arya placed the can of beer on the seat.

"That sounds good," Mila said as she sat on the cool cement slab. She moved the beer over some, and leaned her shoulders against the brick back.

"I'm going to use the thermal camera," Arya said.

"Double and triple checked. The batteries are fully charged," Devon said as he handed the camera to her. "We can begin the session whenever you're ready."

Mila sat upright as Arya worked the camera, watching the small LED screen that was bright with reds, yellows, oranges, dark blues, purples, and black. Each color represented various degrees of temperature.

"I hope you remember us," Mila said into the night while Arya and Devon remained as still and quiet as possible. "I'm here again with my friend, Arya, who has been with me since the beginning. We brought another friend with us. His name is Devon. We think you're trying to communicate with us. Can you talk into the devices with the blinking lights? If you use our energy, we might be able to hear what you have to say."

The group went silent, and the breeze faded away as if the night were holding its breath in anticipation of something big to come.

But the silence responded, and it was louder than a scream.

Devon set the digital recorder on the wide brick arm next to Mila. He spoke while he did so, digitally tagging his movements to help with the analysis they would review the following day.

"This is Devon, and I'm placing the recorder on the arm of the chair."

He dug through the contents of the duffel bag and took out the Ovilus 4 ITC. The Instrumental Trans Communication (ITC) allows for spirit communication through electronic or mechanical means. In a plainer way of describing it, the machine converts environmental readings into voice.

As soon as Devon settled beside Arya, the device spoke rapidly, and the words appeared on the screen. It said:

Message
Chest
Below

"Thank you for that," Arya said. "We are listening."

The team continued to work, calling out to the spirits or whatever was willing to communicate. Almost a half hour went by and they hadn't gotten another response.

"I think we should do a session with the SLS camera," Mila suggested. "And Arya needs to sit here to see if it stirs any response. If it's alright with you, I'd like to run the SLS."

"I think that's a great idea," Devon said. He powered the SLS up, checked it, and handed it to Mila. He said, "Everything looks good. I'll continue to measure and monitor the environment."

Mila moved in front of Arya as she settled into the chair. She looked at Arya through the small LED screen.

"Can you hold my hand?" Arya said into the night, leaning on the arm opposite where Devon placed the recorder. "I want you to know it's OK to use our energy. You have our permission." Arya held her hands out and looked at Mila. "Oh, wow. It's really cold here."

Just as Arya finished the sentence, a stick figure appeared on the SLS screen. It stood next to Arya, appearing to hold her hand.

"Where are you cold?" Mila asked, and that line of questioning got Devon's attention. He hurried to Mila's side and looked at what she was seeing on the small screen.

Arya raised the hand where the stick figure lingered. "This hand," she said as she shook it. "It's freezing. Why, are you seeing something?"

"Yes. Something is next to you where you're feeling the temperature change. I haven't seen this before, but it looks like it's holding your hand."

"Can you tell me your name?" Arya said.

As if it were responding to her questioning, the stick figure disappeared and quickly reappeared next to Arya, but now sitting in the chair with her.

"Keep talking," Devon encouraged. "It seems to be responding to you."

"Is there something you're trying to tell us?"

The ITC rattled off two words:

Under
South

"Thank you," Arya said. "You're doing great."

"Oh my god," Mila said, her eyes wide as she watched the small screen. "This is crazy."

"What is it?" Devon said, then looked to understand. The SLS mapping showed what appeared to be the figure leaning forward, elbows on knees, with their head down. "Amazing."

"I know it's hard, but you're doing great," Arya reiterated. "We want to help you. For us to do that, you have to use our energy and focus it on the machines with the light."

Help
Arya

"Help," Devon said. "It said help Arya."

"What do you want me to help you with?" Arya asked.

The figure stood and vanished.

"Oh!" Mila shouted. "It stood and disappeared!"

"Before you go, can you tell us your name?"

Everyone remained still in hopes of capturing a response or, even better, the figure returning in such a way that the SLS could map it again.

"Alright," Devon said after twenty minutes of inactivity. He began to collect the equipment. "Now that things have slowed down, we can get some baseline readings. That may explain some things."

"I'll grab the K2," Arya said.

"I'm going to stick with the SLS," Mila said.

"Alright," Devon said. "I'll have the digital voice recorder and the FLIR. Maybe we should start with the area where you guys caught the shadow figure?"

"I like that idea," Mila said. "But I think we should keep the Ovilus running because we've gotten so many responses on it."

Devon powered on the Ovilus and rechecked the battery. "It's healthy," he said, handing it to Mila.

Walls

Fire

"Oh! Walls. Fire! Did you hear that?"

"You have to be kidding me," Mila said. "That wasn't even ten seconds and these responses sound intelligent."

"I'm lost for words," Arya said. "The things it's saying have to have meaning."

"We should write out all the words it's saying to see if it makes any sense."

Guide

Metal

Dig

"This is incredible and has been almost nonstop," Mila said.

"I've never had so much activity. I'm actually having a hard time keeping up with it," Devon said. "Is this how it has been?"

"Not to this degree," Arya said. "It seems like every time we come back, the activity increases."

Chapter 8

SPIRIT-GUIDE

The past

Clyde settled on the cot in the hot, darkened room. A single candle on the small, rickety table next to him burned undisturbed, its melted wax running onto the table, pooling and drying in strange designs.

The anger and frustration he felt after he walked Grace to her living quarters and how she closed the door behind her hadn't subsided at all. She simply walked away from him without saying another word. Just like that, the conversation was over. It didn't matter what he thought or what he wanted to convey. It was done. Have a good day, Clyde. See you. Maybe.

"Grace?" he had said as she walked away. "Why won't you talk to me?"

"I'm not interested in hearing what your spirit-guide thinks about me."

Her words had bite, yet upsetting her wasn't his intention. He was trying to understand what was happening but, instead, was getting people's dander up.

"Hang on," Clyde had responded, desperate to keep her attention. "I didn't say it was anything bad."

"Maybe not, but I'll give you some time to figure out why I'm ending this conversation."

The way he was left standing there made him feel insignificant and dumb. He was far from stupid and knew when someone wasn't telling him the truth, and he didn't need a spirit-guide to tell him that. It was even worse because he knew they were hiding something. Either that, or he was just plain paranoid. And he knew he wasn't that.

"George is no good, either," Clyde said into the darkened room. "I don't know what people see in him."

"Strength," a deep voice replied. "Leadership. Vision and resources. Exactly what they need."

Leaning against the wall on the other side of the small room, Clyde saw Odious had his arms folded across his chest. His form wasn't much more than an ebon blot, but the tone in which he spoke to Clyde let him know he was frustrated and maybe even irritated with him.

"I have some thinking to do," Clyde said not much louder than a whisper. "I'm in no mood to go back and forth with you tonight."

"Your mood matters not. And what is there to think about?" Odious sighed. "Look, George suspects something is off with you, and we know he'll keep you at arm's distance until you do something to change that. He will do that until he can figure out what is troubling him. I'm here to tell you that we don't have time for that. You need to do something."

Clyde heaved a sigh and hung his head. "Yeah, I know. I need to figure that out but don't need you to remind me."

"You need me more than ever because you didn't handle that right. You must convince him or anyone else he brings into his 'investigation' that you're not a threat." Odious walked across the room and stared out the dirty window. "I'm not sure how you do that when they have access to otherworldly assistants. Especially since your behavior raised his suspicion."

"Well, I have an otherworldly assistant, too." Clyde paused. "Unless I've really lost myself and gone crazy and you're not here nor ever have been."

"I'm most certainly here, Clyde. You know that."

"So this is fixable. One advantage I have is that Grace told me she hasn't connected with her guide yet. Can you tell if that's true?"

"I've been watching her. She's quite powerful but undeveloped and has a lot of work to do." Odious faced Clyde and his fire-red skin came into focus, aided by the pale moonlight. "It's true. I've watched her working to get her guide's attention. But that connection will need time and nurturing. That's how I was able to step in when she went into the spirit realm to try and make contact with your spirit-guide."

"She did what?"

"Under George's direction. But don't worry. I interfered, timing your arrival at George's place with her interaction in the spirit realm. My timing couldn't have been better, and because of that, you're in the clear for now."

"What about George's guide?"

"Guides. And they're very powerful."

"How many?"

"Almost a dozen."

Clyde shifted. "That's not good."

"No, but I'm doing all I can to mute them, expending a lot of resources. There is one he has an extraordinary connection with. George on his own is strong. Because of his abilities and his guides, he is downright dangerous. I can't keep them in the dark forever. They will figure out a way through our defenses and will expose us."

"That's another cause for concern," Clyde said, contemplating. "I'm not sure if I should remain here or find another camp."

Odious sighed. "You were sent for a very particular reason, and you've been granted great gifts and strength because of that." He paced. "I wouldn't want them to sever our connection and cast you into exile for disobedience. Or me along with you, for that matter."

"No," Clyde said, his uneasiness audible. "Exile is not where I want to be."

"Well, you need to get your act together and do it quickly. Time is not on our side if things aren't corrected."

"It never is, is it? But what if we have a way of changing that? All of this chatter has given me an idea. What is Grace's guide's name?"

"Zippora."

"Could you do what you did when you interfered by making an appearance for Zippora?"

Odious stopped and faced Clyde. If a smile could make a sound, Clyde's ears would've been ringing from the mischievous grin that parted Odious's lips.

"Indeed, I can. I like where this is going. Tell me what you're thinking."

"You're the one who reminded me that George will never trust me. But what if I can get Grace to trust me?"

"She's the weaker link."

Clyde enjoyed a chuckle and clapped his hands. "Exactly. I think we've found our way in and a long-term solution to our problem." He blew out the candle, laid back, and interlaced his fingers behind his head. Heaving a sigh, he closed his eyes. "That's how he will learn to trust me. I'll use what he trusts against him."

"This has been a very productive conversation. It is amazing what happens when you put your mind to something instead of giving in to your frustrations and looking to give up and run away. You're better than that. *We're* better than that. Sweet dreams, Clyde, and rest up. You have a lot of work to do."

Chapter ⑨

ANALYSIS

Present day

"I can't believe how intense that cold was around my hand," Arya said. "It was like I stuck my hand in an icebox. I haven't experienced temperature manipulation like that since . . . well . . ."

Last night, after their hours-long investigation of the Devil's Chair, Arya, Mila, and Devon packed their gear and went straight home. The excitement of the potential evidence they caught had them buzzing, but also exhausted from the heat and adrenaline. With little conversation on the way home, they decided they would meet at ten a.m. They collectively agreed they would take the afternoon and go over all the footage and audio they had collected, then discuss their findings.

"You don't need to say it, Arya," Devon said. "We know."

"Yeah, you would, wouldn't you?" she said, holding up a hand. "Don't answer that, Devon."

"What's going on here?" Mila asked, her eyes volleying between Arya and Devon.

"I don't know," Devon said. "She just bit my head off."

"That's the least you deserve," Arya said.

"You didn't say anything all night. Why are you so mad all of a sudden?"

"How about not commenting about things from the past?"

"I was only trying to help," Devon said. "I didn't want you to feel like you had to elaborate."

"Dev?" Mila said, and he looked at her, his eyes aglow with frustration. "It's OK. Alright?"

"Yeah, sure," he said.

Reviewing evidence was the part most paranormal investigators despised. It was a painstakingly slow process that killed your back from sitting so long, made your eyes tired from staring at a screen all day, and, like many other aspects of the paranormal, made you question your choice of hobbies. They did all this in an attempt to validate their experiences, curiosities, or whatever the motive in an attempt to find the holy grail of evidence that would change the world. Imagine if there were irrefutable proof of the unseen.

Mila hugged Devon and whispered in his ear, "Thank you." She yawned and stretched.

"Yeah," he muttered, getting back to work.

When reviewing footage, if you took your eyes away from the screen for a fraction of a second or daydreamed about what might be for lunch, you could miss what you were working so hard to find. Literally, in some instances, desired footage could last less than a second. It was imperative to stay alert to avoid the aforementioned pitfalls of missing key pieces of evidence.

"Hey, can you guys listen to this and tell me what you hear?" Devon said, unplugging his headphones and adjusting the volume on the external speakers. Mila and Arya paused what they were doing and gave Devon their full attention.

"What are we looking for?" Mila said.

"It's a sound. You're listening for something. Tell me what you hear." Devon played footage from the FLIR camera shot at the chair, and the girls focused on Devon's request.

"Wait," Arya said. "Play that again."

"Are you kidding me?" Mila said at the same time Arya spoke.

"OK, hang on. I'm going to play it again."

In reaction to what they heard, the girls looked at each other.

"That was an obvious cough," Arya said.

"Yeah, it's really loud, too," Mila said.

"A sick cough is how I would describe that," Devon said. "Definitely not an itch in the throat sort of thing. But hang on. There's something else I want to share with you. It's compelling."

Devon pulled up another file, clicked some buttons, and watched the girls with obvious interest. The recording finished playing and they looked at each other, then at Devon.

"I didn't hear anything," Arya said.

"Yeah, what are we missing?"

"That recording I just played is the exact loop, but from the digital recorder. I was running them both simultaneously and they were barely a foot apart."

Arya sat back and shook her head. "Wow. It's like I'm sixteen all over again hearing all these disembodied sounds."

Mila said, "Maybe the time signatures are misaligned?"

"I knew you were going to say that and I'm glad you did," Devon said. He moved the mouse around and clicked some buttons. An MP3 played at the same time as the FLIR video. On the video, Devon spoke, then Mila said something. Right after that, coughing followed. To prove the files were aligned, the exact same sounds came from the digital recorder—but the cough was absent.

"Wow," Mila said. "That's wild. Good catch."

"Yeah, I thought so too and couldn't wait for both of you to hear it," Devon said. He rubbed his eyes, then sat back before he struggled to his feet. "I think my ass is flatter than it normally is if that's possible. I vote for a bathroom break and then we go over what we found?"

"Yes," Mila said and stood. "Don't mind if I do." She wasted no time being the first to go.

"So," Arya said, the irritation in her voice noticeably absent. "Did you find anything else interesting?"

"Quite a few things actually. I'm glad I was able to investigate with you. That place is very active."

"Yeah," Arya said. "And I'm finding myself thinking about it all the time. I want to go back again tonight. It's like I don't care what we caught. I don't feel it's enough and I feel like something is trying to communicate with me, but I haven't heard what it's trying to say yet."

"You're hearing yourself, right?" Devon said. "You need to be careful of that. We don't know if something is trying to attach itself to you or what."

"Or what, what?" Mila said as she entered the room, her eyes going back and forth between Devon and Arya. "Is everything alright?"

"Do you mind if I go next? I really gotta go," Devon said to Arya.

"No, you go ahead," she said. "I can wait."

"She'll tell you," Devon said as he headed out of the room. His voice faded away as he said, "A second opinion is always good."

Mila looked at Arya, brows raised. "Did I step away at the wrong time?"

"No, it's nothing like that. I just feel like something is trying to communicate with me, and whatever that something is, I can't figure out," Arya said. "And it's frustrating me."

"Yet," Mila said, and stared before she waved her hand impatiently. "There's more to it than that. What's the part you left out?"

"I want to go back."

"Hmm," Mila said, scrutinizing Arya. "Do I need to say it?"

She wouldn't look at Mila. "No. Devon already covered it."

"Look at me."

Arya folded her arms and hung her head.

"No, you need to look at me."

Arya did, and her hands wrestled with each other.

"Listen," Mila said. "You were really guarded when we first went there. Whatever's happening, you need to be aware that it's pulling your guard down."

Arya sat upright and pulled her shoulders back. "Yeah, well, I don't think it's negative in any way."

"How do you know?"

"I don't know." She contemplated. "It's just a feeling and nothing is contradicting that."

"Maybe, but we won't let you go back," Devon said as he reentered the room. "Those are the rules and we have to stick to them."

Arya nodded and sighed. "Yeah, I know. I've gotta pee." She walked out of the room.

"Should I go after her?" Mila whispered. "Have a talk with her?"

"No," Devon said and shook his head. "She needs to absorb what she's being told and needs a little bit of space. Not to her degree, but we've all been there and we know it's not easy. She'll make the right decision. She always has."

"Tell her."

Devon nodded. "Maybe now is a good time for a lunch break. It might help reduce the tension. We can continue to review the files after we fill our bellies and clear our heads."

"I think that's a great idea. I'm getting hangry anyways," Mila said.

"All the cuter for it," Devon said.

Arya walked into the room. "Why don't you guys get a room or something?"

"OK by me," Mila said. "Don't threaten me with a good time." She laughed. "I'll call the banana hammock guy for you if you want."

"Good thing I didn't eat yet," Arya said.

Chapter 10

OPPUGN

The past

"I want you to know that I've thought a lot about what you've told me," Clyde said. "I needed to look you in the eye and tell you that I am dedicated to learning and growing through your leadership. I can't express how important this is to me. I don't know what I've done wrong to raise your suspicion or if I'm reading things wrong. Whatever it is, I want to prove my worth and make things right."

George stood with his hands clasped behind his back, looking at Clyde. His expression remained neutral, and he waited patiently for the student to finish speaking.

Clyde continued, "I support you and your vision for the camp and will use my skills to help you build if you'll allow me. Whether that is to swing a hammer or to move piles of wood, I'll do it. It is my hope that I can continue to work on my spiritual growth in the process. Of course, with the support, guidance, and approval under your tutelage."

"Thank you for that," George said. He turned away, covered his mouth, and coughed. He held up a finger, asking for a second. He patted his chest and turned back to face Clyde. "Excuse me. I do feel it is getting better. Although, I'll admit, the itch in my throat is quite fierce."

"Is there anything I can do to help you?"

"With the cough?" George shook his head. "No. But thank you. I know my speech about doing good might have come out of nowhere and seemed harsh, but it is a discussion I must have with every one of my students. Believe it or not, you're not the only one who heard that speech, and you won't be the last. It is not meant to be taken personally, but taken to the heart. We all need to make sure we use our gifts—no matter the stage of growth we are at—for good. I'll accept nothing less, and neither should anyone here. Our goals and intentions need to be respectable."

"Oh thank goodness," Clyde said, heaving a sigh. "I can't tell you how relieved I am to hear you tell me that. Thank you for letting me know. I thought I had done something wrong, but I couldn't figure out what it was. To be honest, I haven't been able to sleep a wink and even asked my guide for assistance. Although I heard no verbal response, I did get guidance."

"Oh? How so?" George asked, smoothing his mustache with a finger as he watched Clyde with a curious eye.

"This isn't the first time he's communicated with me this way. He showed me what he wanted me to know in a dream. It was very clear and there was no room for interpretation. The vision was simply what is happening right now: you and me having a conversation."

"I am glad for that," George said with a smile. "That is invaluable advice and a guide you should make every effort to form an unbreakable bond with. Now, let us make sure we put this to rest once and for all, shall we?"

Clyde nodded.

"Very good," George said. "I would like this done for your sake and my own so we can move on. With that said, I'd like to know if there is anything you need to confess or simply want to talk about?"

"There is nothing," Clyde said. "Not a darn thing." His shoulders drooped and the tension seemed to have lifted.

"That's good and I believe you," George said, clapping Clyde on the back. "I am satisfied with our time together today and feel it was most productive. Trust takes time to build, and these are our first steps toward accomplishing that. Now, I would like to show you something important to me."

George could feel Clyde's eyes on him as he moved around his room, looking for something he wanted to share with him. "Ah, here it is." He revealed a large, rolled-up piece of paper pulled from a pile of things. He placed it on the table and opened it, revealing a crude map.

He took his time to smooth out the wrinkles and moved the candle-light so Clyde could see it without shadow. "This is the idea I had for the camp." He revealed a small stack of individual blueprints. "Here are the concepts for the members' housing and the auditorium. In the near future we will construct a hotel. I have plans for that here, too." He pointed at the pile. "But right now, the housing and auditorium come first. More details will follow, but this is the beginning phase. I'm finding myself far too curious to know what you think?"

Clyde rested a hand on top of the table and used his other hand to point as he moved from house to house on the map, the suggested paths by foot and carriage, and the lake area where the camp members could gather.

"This is ambitious."

George nodded. "Is that good or bad? As you were looking for my feedback, I am now looking for yours."

Clyde stood upright and looked at George. "This is great! I mean, simply wonderful. Exciting, too."

"A lot of work has gone into the planning phase, and exactly what you said is what my hope is for everyone. We will be starting construction soon. I feel we need to focus on the auditorium first," George said. "Your thoughts?"

"Oh, I agree," Clyde said, holding a finger on the placement of the auditorium. Its suggested design was an octagon, the building materials wood. "For now, we all have suitable temporary living quarters and nothing in the way of the auditorium. That is an important enhancement. A place for everyone to gather inside a shelter would be beneficial. Having a place we can host church services and conduct séances, workshops, fund-raisers, and even public lectures is important to our continued growth and messaging. I also think it would make this feel more like a community."

"I'm not sure if we should include a verandah with the auditorium," George said.

"I think simple would be better. Does that need to be decided now?"

"Thankfully not," George said. "But I feel our spiritual meeting hall needs to be accessible to all. Inviting. I think it essential we practice together, encourage positive outward energy, and grace our land and community with a frequency that would be strong and resistant to anything negative. Then our focus can shift to the surrounding buildings and houses."

"I couldn't agree more. This is really exciting," Clyde said, poking the map with a stiff finger. "If you'd like, I could start laying out some of the other building plans. Perhaps I can start with your living quarters?" Clyde's eyes were wide with ideas. He calmed himself and stood upright. "I say this with the utmost respect, but I think you deserve a much better home than this and what's on those plans."

"I appreciate your willingness to help."

"I will fully incorporate so people know it was your—"

"I'm not worried about credit," George said with a chuckle. "Your input would be most welcomed, and we don't package anything as my idea. This community is for everyone who will have it and honor it."

"I will do both! I'll start on it tonight and hopefully will have something to show you in a few days. This is very exciting!"

"I appreciate your enthusiasm. It certainly makes all the effort put forth so far well worth it." George grinned, a subtle cough threatening to fill the room in an uncontrolled fit, but he managed to stifle it. "And jot down any other ideas you might have. Roads, paths, layouts. Whatever might come to mind. Remember that we don't have an unlimited budget, so of course, cost is a concern."

"I can do that, and I understand." Clyde extended a hand. "I appreciate you having me here, George. This is the best day I've had since I arrived a few months ago. Thank you. I won't disappoint you."

"I believe that," George said and shook Clyde's hand. He opened the front door. "Have a good rest of your night, and I'll see you tomorrow at the fundraiser."

Clyde walked out into the night, and George closed the door and retreated to the table. He folded the map and drummed his fingers on the tabletop as he slipped into deep thought.

There was something off about Clyde that he couldn't properly finger. This was one of the most frustrating things to occur over the past several years, at least only slightly ahead of the constant itch in his chest that had only recently begun to concern and irritate him equally.

He figured if he opened up to Clyde, it might get Clyde to open up in return, allowing George to get information easily. But it hadn't work.

Clyde's aura had no color, and for George, it was rare that he couldn't read someone. Having spirit-guides that remained as baffled as he was added another layer of concern, curiosity, and determination to understand what it was he couldn't discern. After all, discernment was enlightenment.

He had to admit that asking Clyde to leave would be the easiest solution. Pack your bags and go. But on what grounds would he dismiss him? Suspicion wasn't enough. What if he were sending someone away who had no ill intent and who needed the assistance and guidance of the community? Perhaps a snap judgment was what pushed them into the wrong hands. Then what? The resulting damage could potentially be irreversible and catastrophic.

"To use only for good," George reminded himself. "Especially for me. It must start there. Self-discipline is not only necessary, but a non-negotiable precondition."

George didn't want to take any chances with judging someone without firm evidence. A gut feeling wasn't enough. And, of course, he didn't want anything negative on his conscience or connected to the camp. Karma was real.

It was settled then.

Casting someone out without reason and evidence (rather than a feeling) could be far worse than dealing with a bad seed.

"Ahh, Seneca, I can surely use your help on this one."

George crossed his legs and settled into the chair. The only response his request received was the creak of the wooden chair under his body weight.

"The walls," George heard, the voice sudden and booming. Yet the sound of the voice wasn't audible to the human ear; rather, someone spoke into his subconsciousness.

"What walls?" George said out loud, closing his eyes. He concentrated.

"Oppugn," the response came, the amplification of the voice fading, the tone futile.

"What do you mean?" George asked. "Help me understand what you're trying to tell me."

No answer came, and whoever delivered that message was gone as fast as they had come.

Chapter 00

WIDE AWAKE

The recent past

Arya lifted the covers to her chin. They were her only protection from the thing in her room, tormenting her night after night. It lumbered around, bumping into things, and it grunted incoherently. Whatever this thing was, it didn't care about being noticed.

Thump.

There it was again. She eyed the door, measuring her ability to outrun it. Perhaps she should take a look to see what it was. If it were a cheetah or a coyote, she wouldn't stand a chance because it would be on her in seconds. But she doubted that what was haunting her was an animal—at least not the four-legged kind.

Pulling the covers down ever so slightly, she spied the ebon room. Standing in the far corner, seeming to watch her, was what she perceived to be a person in shadow. It looked tall and wide, and she was certain it was male.

"Can you hear me?"

Arya stiffened. That wasn't her brother's voice, and her father hadn't been home in a long time. In that instant, all of her planning evaporated, and she pulled the covers over her head and curled into a ball. "Please go away," she said, unable to control the fear that now consumed her.

"Wait, you can hear me?" the man wheezed. "I think I'm lost."

Arya wrestled with the desire to get up and run, but she didn't know if her legs would work. Fear was a great controller and she was under its spell. So she lay still and tried to listen, but the thundering of her own heart filled her ears.

"I need your—"

"No!" she shouted, slapping her hands over her ears. She waited a minute and then uncovered her ears and listened. The first thing she noticed was that the sounds within the room fell eerily silent. So she waited, knowing something always happened. Seconds felt like minutes, and the fear intensified to the point of desperation.

The edge of her bed sank, as if someone was sitting down. Arya scrambled out of her cocoon with a gasp and ran out of her room, down the hallway, and into Devon's room. He sat up fast, and Arya dove into his bed, seeking his protection.

"You scared the shit out of me, Arya," Devon said, his face scrunched from sleep. "What the hell are you doing?"

Arya couldn't get close enough to her brother. He was older by a few years and was much bigger and stronger than her. He was brave, too, and probably wouldn't have run from whatever that was. But running was the only thing she could do.

"You can't keep waking me up because you're having bad dreams."

"Who else do I go to?" she said, clinging to his leg. "No one else is here, Devon. In case you forgot, Mom is—"

"Still at work. She's trying to provide," he said as he pried her grip loose. He sat up and rubbed his face. "I don't know why you sound so angry when you mention her. It's like when you say her name, it's dripping with disappointment. All she asks is that we do well in school and keep the house clean. I can't think straight at school half the time because I'm so damn tired. You've had me up at all sorts of hours over the past few months. You can't keep doing this."

"It hasn't been that long."

"I don't think you realize how often this is happening." Devon stood and sighed. "Things have really escalated since Dad left."

"I don't think he left," she whispered, then said, "and I'm not having bad dreams."

"You can mumble all you want. I heard what you said, and yes, you are. You're sad about Dad and you're trying to understand. I don't know, maybe you feel unsafe with him not being here."

"They're not dreams."

"Well then, maybe you're seeing things. I saw something about hypno-whatever dreams, where you get paralyzed."

"I didn't say anything about not being able to move," Arya said, an element of distaste in her inflection. "That means you're looking things up and trying to figure out what's happening to me."

"Of course I am. You're my sister and I care about you."

Arya got out of bed, her fear of the apparition now gone, replaced by a simmering anger at being told that what she was experiencing wasn't real. "You can't look up what you think is happening to me and get real answers. These things aren't made up, and they aren't from an overactive imagination. If they were, then explain to me how it spoke to me and its voice echoed around the room."

Devon rolled his eyes. "Great, now you're hearing things, too. I'm trying to be supportive—I really am. At what point do I put my foot down?"

"I don't get it. Why don't you believe me?"

Devon shook his head and exited his room.

"Where are you going?" Arya asked.

"I'm checking your room. You can come if you want, or you can stay if you don't want to."

"I don't want to go in there."

"That's fine. I'll be back in a minute."

"Devon?"

He stopped and looked at her. "Yes?"

"I saw it and heard it," she said, looking away from his anger and disappointment. "It heard me and it responded. Maybe I'm going crazy, but the one thing I'm not doing is lying."

"I don't believe you're lying," Devon said as he walked down the hallway toward Arya's room. "But I believe you think you saw a ghost and heard one. But you didn't because there is no such thing."

Arya sighed and plopped herself on the foot of Devon's bed. "Great," she whispered, sighed, and looked around the room. It felt different in his room. Like this part of the house was safe.

Devon entered the room with Arya's pillow in his hand. He tossed it at her. "You can sleep on the bottom of my bed for tonight. We can talk about it in the morning."

"Like we got the chance to do with Dad? It's always tomorrow until it doesn't come."

Devon stood there, his expression contorted into something unpleasant. "I don't know what to do." He opened his arms and slapped his thighs, his eyes shifting with indecision. "Maybe we should bring Mom into this."

"No."

"I don't think it's just your decision to make. Of course you're going to say no. You have to see things from my perspective. Something bigger than us is happening, and maybe she can help."

Arya shook her head. "She'll push me away faster than you're doing right now."

"That's not fair." Devon lay down. "Tell me what you want me to do, Arya. What can I do to help?"

"You can start by believing me. Everything I've said is the truth."

"Including what you told me about Mom?"

Arya moved closest to the wall and lay down. She didn't mind his feet in her face. "Yes. It is all true. I heard it with my own ears."

"I find that hard to believe."

"Of course you do," she said. "Because you're treated differently than I am. She's careful when you're around. Whether you believe it or not, whenever she hears about these, they remind her of him and she hates me for it for whatever reason."

"I don't believe that's true," Devon said. "I can't believe that's true." He shifted around until he got comfortable. "We can't solve any of these issues tonight. Like I said, we'll talk about it tomorrow. We both have a long day ahead of us. Try and get some sleep."

Chapter ①②

MANIPULATION

The past

Clyde walked through the wet grass and took a deep breath. He loved the smell of freshly fallen rain, and the break in the heat was noticeable and appreciated. Green tree frogs chattered away, and the pitter-patter of the falling rain blended harmoniously with all the other sounds, creating the perfect soundtrack of Mother Nature's beauty.

Clyde focused on his interaction with George and the feeling he came away with. He believed the conversation had gone way better than he had anticipated. There was little doubt that George now had a greater understanding of what his plight was and seemed more relaxed about his inclusion in the community, and for that, Clyde was thankful and, if he was to be honest with himself, relieved.

"I don't think he suspects anything," he whispered, pumping his fists in celebration. "Whatever had him curious, I think it's gone now."

He knew the promises he had made to George, and the enthusiasm he had shown pertaining to the future of the camp couldn't end with just words. There needed to be follow-up by *doing*. But, he noted, while he did, he could continue to expand on his plans and execute them in secret until his obligation was met.

Then, in a bizarre turn of events, a sudden inexplicable sadness came over him.

"That's odd," he said, trying to dismiss it, but the feeling remained and then began to morph into something much heavier.

In a strange and unexpected way, he was excited about George's plans—truly excited. To imagine how thrilling it would be to live in the colony when everything was done would be nothing short of exhilarating. A self-sustaining thriving community set in a picturesque backdrop with few things around to interrupt their way of life was enticing. It created a sense of belonging and a clear purpose, which was something he never had before.

"No," he said, and he shook his head in defiance. The joy began to fragment as he continued to resist. His purpose of being there was to obstruct George's plans every step of the way, and distractions weren't allowed unless it was to further his plight. And whatever was trying to divert his attention was the work of his enemy.

"Clyde?"

Yanked from the consuming reverie, Clyde's body trembled as he turned to see Grace standing up from the trunk of a fallen tree she had been sitting on. Concealed by the darkness and the cover of other palm trees, she approached Clyde with a wide smile.

"I'm sorry," she said. "I understand now how easy it is to frighten someone while they are in thought, no doubt in appreciation of the beautiful things around them." She looked around in her own appreciation, and said, "I think the location lures you into a sense of security and wonder. It can be quite intoxicating and disruptive. For that, I want to apologize for the way I reacted and spoke to you the other night."

"Wow," Clyde said. "Thank you for that. When I frightened you, it wasn't on purpose. I felt bad, but the way you reacted was off-putting."

"I know that now," Grace said, reaching to touch his hand. "And I am very sorry. Can you forgive me?"

"Of course," Clyde said, looking at her fingers touching his skin. It felt good, but it was just another distraction. "Where are my manners? Yes, of course I can do that."

"That makes me feel better." She withdrew her hand. "I was hoping to catch you before you went inside for the night. The rain brought in some cooler air and it's doing a wonderful job of keeping the bugs away for now. I don't think there has been a more perfect night to enjoy the outdoors in a while." She drew a deep breath and slowly blew it out. "You know, I'm in love with this place, Clyde."

"I am too," Clyde said. "It's peaceful and holds the promise of something great. I want you to know I met with George. We talked about the way I felt and the way he felt."

"And?"

Clyde sighed, placing his hands on his hips and nodding with a smile. "Thankfully, it all went very well," he said as he relaxed. "It seems the tension I felt was nothing more than a misunderstanding. Whatever it was, it's in the past. I am looking forward to and couldn't be more excited for the future."

"That's great news! It seems as though our focus and desires have aligned."

"I had no doubt that they would," Clyde said. "Among the things we already spoke about, I was expecting to have to explain myself to George about frightening you. I feared I had upset you so that you would've told him you didn't want me around any longer. Although I am relieved you didn't, do you mind telling me why you didn't tell George about our interaction?"

"I don't know." Grace shrugged. "I thought about it and didn't think you were lying about why you wanted to speak to me. You had sincerity in your eyes, and you deserve to speak how you feel. It's unfortunate what miscommunication can do. When I went inside for the night, I thought you were a genuinely nice guy. Albeit misunderstood at the moment, but nice."

"Well, jeez," Clyde said as his foot pushed around pebbles. "That was unexpected. I don't know what to say."

"About that? As far as I'm concerned, neither of us needs to discuss it ever again. It was an unfortunate interaction that seemed to have a positive outcome for all of us."

Clyde smiled. "Just like that?"

"Water under the bridge," she said, falling into silence. "So you said something to me today at the fundraiser that I can't get out of my mind." She settled in front of him. He was much taller than she was, and being she was standing so close, her head was tilted all the way back. "You said something about my spirit-guide?"

"Oh yes," Clyde said and began to walk toward his living quarters. This action was purposeful, like he was dragging a line with bait on a hook through the water, and Grace was a hungry fish, oblivious of the pole and line that would rip her from her world.

"Were you being serious?" Grace asked, following the scent of something appetizing just ahead.

"I most certainly was," he said, choosing his words carefully, making his promises believable, his intention seeming pure. *Bite the hook!*

"Do you have the time to talk about how you could get me to establish a connection with my spirit-guide?"

"It's not that I don't have the time. I wasn't planning on doing much of anything right now," Clyde said. "I'm a little bit tired and was looking forward to relaxing after having that talk with George. I feel like a giant weight has been lifted off my shoulders and, as a side effect of that release, I'm surprised how tired I feel."

Now I have you.

"Oh," Grace said. Her response dripped with disappointment. "I needed time to absorb what you were telling me but probably should have accepted your offer right then. But if I'm to be forthright, I didn't know how to respond at the time. I was reluctant to accept your offer because the thought of it makes me nervous. As I continued to think about it, I became more and more curious about how that connection could be made. And then, well, here I am. I had hoped you'd still be willing to help me."

Clyde continued to walk to his place, Grace only half a stride behind him. He smirked, purposely towing that invisible line. Maybe now, while her mouth was closing around the hook, he needed to give it a gentle tug to set it.

"Of course I'd be willing to help you, Grace. We can go to your place or to mine," Clyde said. "I don't want you to be disappointed, and I want you to establish a connection with your guide. Your growth is important to me and the community."

"Bless your heart. We can go wherever you prefer," Grace said. "Wherever you think is better."

"Alright," Clyde said with a smirk, knowing she didn't bite the hook, she swallowed it! "Let's go to my place. The energy there is calibrated to me, and I work on fine-tuning it every day. I think we would have more success there."

Grace put a gentle hand on Clyde's shoulder. "Thank you for doing this. I appreciate your willingness to help me more than I can ever say."

Clyde chased away the smile that threatened to give away his ploy. He looked at Grace. He couldn't have planned things any better. What was to come would solidify her loyalty and belief in him. Clyde exaggerated a sigh. "I don't mind at all. In fact, your desire to get this started is inspiring me. I might as well put this second wind to good use."

Grace skipped with joy and danced around him. "I'm so excited! Thank you, Clyde."

Clyde sat cross-legged in the middle of the room and held hands with Grace. Two dimly lit candles and a perfect circle created from crushed chalk were located in the center of the room. The furniture was pushed to the walls, and the windows were stuffed with newspaper, blocking out any interference from the moonlight and moving clouds that might give the impression of someone or something moving throughout the room.

"Are you ready?" Clyde asked, squeezing Grace's hands.

She nodded. "I am."

"When I asked my spirit-guide about you last night, he said he was in contact with yours. He told me that if you concentrate and focus with all your heart and all your strength, your guide has the ability to come through. The veil that separates you is thin, that the link could be made at last."

Grace shivered.

"Don't fret. This is a good thing," Clyde said. "Relax and try to make that connection. If you wish it to happen, it will. Now, let's concentrate."

A long moment of silence engulfed the room, Clyde and Grace remained still with their eyes closed. Soon, their shoulders went limp and the candlelight seemed to dim, the room consumed in absolute silence. The sound of breath and the normal creaking of the temporary living quarters were stifled.

"Spirits and spirit-guides, we look to connect with Grace's guide and only her guide tonight," Clyde said. "If you hear our voice, can you please come forward and let your presence be known."

The candles flickered and, somewhere above, something cracked.

"That is a sign and we thank you for that," Clyde said, holding Grace's hands firmly. She looked to withdraw her hold, but Clyde took control and squeezed her hands, rubbing the tops of them with his thumbs, letting her know everything was alright.

"A name," Clyde said, his closed eyelids twitching as he searched for the next answer. "We are looking to make a connection, to begin the bond between you and Grace this evening. You indicated you wanted to and that is why we're here."

In the distance, a long, rolling thunder scraped the sky, making Grace stiffen again. Clyde clamped down to let her know there was nothing to fear. It was all a part of the process.

"Zip," Clyde said, and Grace gasped and withdrew before Clyde could restrain her.

Grace stared at him, and Clyde said, "Are you OK?"

The dancing candlelight was ominous and the atmosphere thin. The shadows that morphed looked like a judging audience, and the silence felt like nothing more than the calm before shouts of judgment.

"Grace, you need to answer me! Are you OK?"

Grace looked around and Clyde watched her. He noticed she entered the variance. Once in there, the shadows and the ambiance didn't look chaotic. Somehow, this unexplainable shift they were in the center of made perfect sense. Driven by calmness, she looked around a second time and seemed to receive the same inference.

Grace drew a deep breath and sighed. "Yes, I am OK. This is new and I was afraid, but I'm not anymore. I think I understand. Let's continue."

"Are you sure?"

"I am certain," she said and closed her eyes. Her voice lowered to a faint whisper. "I have never been so sure."

"Zip," Clyde said after a brief pause to reset the room. "What are your intentions?"

A long, confusing silence sat between the two, the energy high. Clyde lowered Grace's hands to her knees and set his gentle touch on top of hers. "Help her know who you are."

Another long, strained beat stayed in the room.

"Use our energies to let her know you are here and give her your full name."

Thump.

Silence.

The candles went out.

"Who?" Clyde said, searching, demanding.

Another thump.

The candles relit.

"Zippora, I hear you," Clyde finally said. "Thank you. It is not me you seek."

Grace went to stand, but Clyde reached forward and encouraged her to stay.

"Not me, but she is here for you," he said, holding her hands to her knees. "She wants to make a connection." He whispered, "Relax, Grace. Don't break the circle of trust."

"Oh," Grace said as the connection was fully made. "It is beautiful. Oh my God, it is so beautiful! There are no words to describe this."

She lay back and Clyde lowered her down gently. He grabbed a pillow and placed it behind her head. Her spirit-guide took over and brought her to a place where the lines of connection could be firmly established.

"Grace?"

Grace twitched at the surprising clarity with which the voice came to her. It was near, but behind. She turned to see a pleasant-faced woman with deep-set eyes. Standing at only five feet tall with black hair that hung at shoulder length, she looked at Grace in earnest.

"I am Grace," she said or thought, and at this moment, she didn't know the difference. She wasn't exactly sure how this interaction worked. "Are you—"

"I am Zippora," the woman said as a pleasant smile spread across her lips and showed her teeth. She gleamed with delight, and the positive energy she exuded was contagious. "I am your spirit-guide, and I've been working long and hard to establish a connection with you."

Grace's eyes welled with tears. This moment was better than any in her twenty-four years of life. The smile that overtook her matched Zippora's. "And I have been trying to reach you for as long as I can remember. I always sensed your presence and how you were encouraging me to not give up. I promised myself that if I ever had a chance to converse with you, I would tell you all the things I've needed to say." She laughed. "The funny thing is, now that we are speaking, I can't remember a single thing I wanted to tell you."

Zippora shared a laugh. "That's the way things go. It doesn't matter, really. What you know, I will know. Besides, I have much to tell you as well. Now that the connection between us has been established, we have plenty of time to communicate and to get to know each other. In due time, I'm sure you'll remember some of the things you've wanted to tell me, and if you do, we can share it then."

Zippora's form dimmed and faded away.

"Zippora?"

Grace ran in the direction Zippora had dissipated, her eyes searching the impossible darkness she found herself in.

"Zippora!" she shouted, her voice straining. Widened eyes struggled to capture any light so she could see what was happening, but the darkness held onto its secret.

"Grace," a voice said, the tone deep and haunting. Threatening even.

"Who is there?" she said, continuing her desperate search of the darkness. That wasn't Zippora. The hairs on Grace's arms stood.

"Stop and look. You will see."

Grace stopped and looked. Two small red dots were hovering about fifteen feet away. There was no question that those were the eyes of something sinister looking back at her. A diabolical laugh bellowed all around her. As they made the link, the area she occupied bounced sound around as though they occupied a small, hollow room.

"Come forward, and let's talk."

Grace hesitated.

"Don't listen to that thing," Zippora said, sprinting out of the darkness. "It's sent by the devil himself!"

Grace heard the collision of their bodies, and then the eyes were no longer visible. A brief tussle followed and Zippora came into view.

"What happened?" Grace said, her confusion evident. "How can I help you?"

Zippora grabbed Grace's hand and looked deeply into her eyes. "Continue to hone your skills and allow me to guide you."

"But the demon!"

"That is my worry and the guide that aids me."

"Wait. Your guide?"

Zippora let out an innocent giggle and nodded as she did so. "Things are very different here. Spiritual warfare is everywhere and on many different levels of reality. But that is a lesson for another time." She squeezed Grace's hands. "Hone your skills. It is time for you to go. Now, you need to wake up!"

Grace sat up and gasped for air. Clyde was kneeling next to her, patting her back and holding her by the arm.

"You're OK, breathe," he said. "Easy."

"I saw . . . I saw her . . ."

"Shh, don't talk. Catch your breath and gather your energy."

"She was in conflict with a demon."

"Shh," Clyde said. "Your awareness is growing, Grace. I think you're now aware that not everything we do is glorious. Our guides are constantly being challenged and attacked like we are. It would be foolish to think people are the only ones under assault."

Chapter ①❷③

BITTER TRUTH

The recent past

Arya leaned her back against the wall and sobbed. Her eighteen-year-old mind raced with the details of the past hour, and she always found herself searching for an understanding of something that couldn't be understood. She saw and heard things other people couldn't comprehend and, although it had been going on for years, everything about it was frightening and it didn't get any easier.

She didn't know why, but people who had died would come to her and make her feel what they felt. Chest pains from someone who had a heart attack, severe belly pains from a young woman who had been stabbed to death, and, one time, she felt like she was in an emotional fog. This was an indicator that the elderly person who vied for her attention had suffered from some sort of memory disease and they needed her help navigating the other side. But she didn't have the skills to help anyone, and when she told them they had the wrong person, they wouldn't listen. Night after night they came, seeking her guidance. It had become overwhelming and it interfered in every part of her life.

Over the past year she'd worked hard at shutting these things out and looked to protect herself. It was only natural to try and eliminate that which afflicted her, not satisfied with her self-diagnosis that she was either crazy or somehow cursed. Some people thought these abilities could be a gift—even glorified them—but having lived it, Arya could attest to the fact that those notions were the furthest things from the truth.

The past month, she had a handful of vivid dreams where someone from the past interacted with her. She figured it was someone from over one hundred years ago. Unfamiliar with the type of clothing they wore, she'd seen pictures from the early nineteen hundreds, and that's where she placed them from. This person was a pleasant-faced woman.

At first, the dreams were charming. A breezy, cool day. Delightful smells. The woman held a book, had meaningless chatter with other faceless people who stopped by as she rocked gently on a porch. Then things darkened. The woman was killed from behind, possibly a knife in the back, as shadowy fingers covered her mouth and her eyes opened wide, surprised by the sharp steel that took her life. Then angels and demons fought among hellfire, souls in an eternal, invisible struggle.

Arya didn't want to see these distressing events, and the desperate feeling of needing to get away filled her with panic. No matter how hard she tried to escape, something unseen kept her there in a manner she couldn't grasp, facilitating the slow approach of her own demise. The most dreadful part of these dreams was how she couldn't see what was containing her, but she could feel it, and it was wicked and more abhorrent than the things she was seeing.

And tonight, although it had nothing to do with the woman she often saw but hadn't seen since her execution, things escalated to a level Arya had never experienced before. This night, she saw the physical manifestation of a person, or what she perceived to be a person, form in her bedroom. The temperature in the room plummeted, but Arya was unsure if the shivering was brought on by the cold or the sudden appearance of the almost solid figure. What she did know was that she was terrified. The form watched her, accompanied by a vile aura, and as soon as it became aware of her consciousness, it shouted something ghastly, its words not English, and it lunged at her. That's when she ran for safety.

As she stood there, contemplating these things outside the door of her bedroom, the knowledge of this evil clung to her and wouldn't withdraw. It was like it wanted her to know it and fear it and never forget it. As much as she didn't want to remember these details, the interaction and lingering dread that made her heart race clung to her with an unbreakable clasp.

"What's going on?" Devon said, coming out of his bedroom.

"I had a bad dream," Arya said, her body trembling.

Her brother looked at her and seemed annoyed. "So you decided to come out into the hallway?"

"Well, yeah," she said as she looked at him, annoyed. "I'm freaked out!"

"You're breathing really heavy. Like you ran a mile. It's loud enough that you woke me up."

"Yeah," Arya said. "I see that. I'm sorry, but it felt so real and I needed to get out of there."

He rubbed his eyes. "You said it was just a dream."

"Yeah, that's what I said," she whispered and turned her head away. "I don't know, maybe it was something more than that."

"What do you mean?"

"We're going to go through this again?"

"What did you mean by that, Arya?"

"I saw something. In my room. It had a physical form. I could feel its presence and it wasn't pleasant. I swear, if I had wanted to touch it, I could have."

Devon shook his head. "You're telling me you saw someone standing in your room?"

"Yes, I think so." She whispered, "I don't know," and after a moment said, "It was really dark. It looked like the shadow of a person. Maybe it was the thing with the lady on the porch."

"What porch?"

"Never mind."

"I am minding." Devon walked into her room and looked around. "This goes on constantly. I want to show you that it was just a dream, Arya. It might've been scary, but it was just a dream."

"It's not like it's going to stick around and wait for you. You can't tell me that all of these interactions are the result of an overactive imagination. And you don't have to make me feel like an idiot."

"And maybe you could've stayed in your room! I don't know, maybe you need to tell Mom that the nightmares are coming back."

"Absolutely not. It was one dream." Arya wiped away her tears and folded her arms. "The last time someone told Mom, they turned me into a zombie, Devon. Don't you remember what I was like?"

"Yeah, I remember."

"You should, because you're the one who told her."

"That's not fair," Devon said. "I was only trying to help you."

"I'm not taking pills and I'm not telling Mom anything and neither are you. I actually saw something standing in my room with my own eyes. You don't have to believe me—that's fine. I know what I saw."

Devon stared at her. "What am I supposed to do?"

"You don't understand."

"No, I guess I don't."

"Well, I can't help you like you can't help me. And I'm not kidding. Don't say anything to Mom," Arya said. "It's not your place. You've already overstepped once, so don't ever do it again."

He scratched his head and turned away. "Yeah, OK, sure. Can you at least try keeping it down? I have finals tomorrow and I'm really tired. College isn't easy. I thought someone broke into the house. Now you have me wide awake. I hope I can fall back asleep."

"Yeah, I chose not to go to college, so somehow I'm less than you."

"You're being ridiculous."

"Of course I am," she said as she watched him go into his room and shut the door. "No, I'll be fine, thanks for asking," she whispered, turning to look at her room. It was a darkened maw, ready to eat her if she dared to enter it again. It was a warning she would heed and found it best to retreat to the sofa for the rest of the night. She hoped to wake up before her mother got home from working the night shift. Unquestionably, anything Mom deemed to be out of the ordinary always stirred her curiosity, and it turned into an interrogation and a knockdown, drag-out argument.

"Maybe I'm just not compatible with that room," she reasoned as she headed to the couch. "It could be that my energy clashes with whatever energy is there." She lay down on her back, her eyes wide open, her mind fully awake. "I'll ask him if he wants to change rooms with me. Maybe that will help."

Chapter ⑪

LATH AND PLASTER

The past

Clyde took special care in making sure each strip of thin wood was nailed in straight rows to the vertical beams, spaced a perfect quarter inch apart. He was more proficient in working with laths than he originally pitched himself to George. It was far better to show what you can do rather than to talk about it. That was an old rule he often stuck by— show, don't tell.

"I didn't know you were this good," George said, a smile parting his lips as he admired Clyde's work. He twirled the end of his mustache, stopped, and then looked at Clyde. "Probably the best I've ever seen."

"Ah, thank you," Clyde said as he continued to work. He applied plaster in thick gobs to the lath, pressing it firmly into the wooden slats, knowing the seepage on the inside of the wall created keys. Keys, when dried, were what gripped the plaster to the wooden boards for strength. "If you're impressed by my work, you should see the skilled hands of the men who taught me."

"Perhaps we should send an express mail message to your friends? Maybe we could entice them to apply their skills, and we can aid in their spiritual growth while they do so?" George paused again while he admired Clyde's work. "Spiritual growth is much more valuable than coins."

"To be reunited with them would be amazing," Clyde said. "But somehow bad luck wriggled its way into the projects we were working on together. Misfortune and illness devastated everyone. As strange as it might sound, there were rumblings of a curse. It was all quite daunting, and even now, it is difficult to talk about."

"I'm so sorry to hear that. I won't press," George said. "Really, I need to tell you how impressed I am with your work, Clyde. Perhaps you'd like to oversee the quality of the builds as I finish plans for the remaining layouts? I won't deny that this cough has taken a lot out of me. I could use your help."

Clyde exaggerated some final touches and made no attempt to hide his joy. "I would be honored," he said, extending a hand stained with the day's hard, laborious work. "But on one condition."

"I'm listening."

"You take the opportunity to slow down a little. This should allow you to rest so you can heal properly."

"I don't want to, but I understand why I have to."

"So we're in agreeance," Clyde said. "I won't disappoint you."

George looked around the unfinished room. "I know you won't," he said, shaking Clyde's hand. He inspected the framing, floor, and wall, seeing it all coming together. The two-story home Clyde insisted George have was exciting, and if it turned out half as good as the auditorium, he'd never have to worry about shelter again.

"Say, George?"

"Yeah, Clyde?" George coughed and turned away. "Excuse me."

"I don't need to explain why I requested you to slow down and rest."

"No, you don't."

"I don't like the sound of that cough. I've been telling you that for almost three weeks now, and regardless of what you say, it doesn't sound like it's getting better."

"I know you don't, and I do appreciate your honesty and concern. I don't like it either."

"It has been going on for far too long."

"I know my body is trying to fight it off because I feel very worn down today."

"The medicine you're taking is helping to manage it, but you don't sound any better. Perhaps there is a different remedy available to you?" Clyde paused, eyeing George with a look of concern. "Something to think about. Anyway, would you approve of my leveraging an assistant?"

George folded his arms. "Meaning?"

"I'm thinking maybe Grace could help me move things along smoothly and quickly. She has a splendid eye for detail, is organized, and doesn't take anything from anyone."

"Did I just hear you request Grace?"

Clyde nodded, slow and thoughtful, just like his work. "I could give her the basics so I wouldn't have to be bogged down with the smaller details. Her skills are untapped, and I think she could be really helpful."

George pulled at his chin. "I'm not sure she would be interested in this, being that this is perceived as work for men."

"She wouldn't be in the trenches, and will help keep me there. The worst she could say is an emphatic no. And if you don't mind, I would like to ask her. I don't want to have it coming from you where she feels she has to do it. I want the choice to be hers."

George nodded. "If you think it's beneficial, I'm not opposed."

"To be forthright, I've been watching her in class for a while now, and I think her communication skills are a step above the others. I'm not talking about her spiritual growth, although that is important. I'm talking about her excellent forewoman skills. They could be put to good use out here as well."

George's arms fell to his sides as he reviewed the work unfolding around him. "Darn, everything is coming out exactly as I envisioned it. I'm sold and you don't have to try and convince me. If you think her skills can help move this along faster by freeing you up, then I give you a resounding yes as long as she agrees."

"Very good," Clyde said. "I, like you, can spot talent from a mile away." He smirked. "At least I believe I can. I suppose I'll put my watchful eye to the test for the first time."

"I'll tell you what. If she says yes, why don't you both come by my quarters tonight to have a toast."

"That sounds great."

"Say, seven o'clock?"

"I'll be there and hopefully with good news." Clyde scooped a large, thick pile of plaster onto a board he held in his left hand. "I'm looking to finish this wall before I talk to her, so I better get a move on if I want to be able to pop the question and get to your house on time." He began to spread the plaster over the lath, building thick, smooth layers like an artist with a canvas and brush.

"I hope to see you both at seven then," George said, then clapped Clyde on the back and then exited the new construct with a sense of attainment.

Everything was coming along exactly as he had planned.

Clyde worked the plaster to keep it from setting. He watched George as he walked away, a deep cough departing with him. Clyde couldn't help but feel good about the conversation they just had. He felt as though he was slowly taking control and gaining the trust of the one person he needed on his side.

"Yeah, I look forward to seeing you later," Clyde said under his breath, turning his attention to the wall. George was right—everything was coming out just as planned. But not according to just his plan. There were other things at work.

Everything good needed an element of bad, and, of course, anything bad needed to flourish and grow. That flourishing and growth could only thrive by devouring anything that was deemed positive.

"Speaking of which," Clyde whispered, digging his hand into his pocket. He withdrew a folded piece of paper and looked around to make sure he wasn't being watched. Everyone was busy, going about completing their assigned work, not paying attention to him in the least.

He unfolded the paper and looked at the incantation he and Odious had written together last night. A spell to help break the positivity and introduce havoc. A spell to help bind Grace's guide and confuse her, keeping her away for good. The first spell wasn't intended to cause widespread immediate chaos, but rather release it in a controlled drip.

"A seed to grow."

Clyde dropped the paper into the wall and watched it as it fell to the bottom. He closed his eyes and recited a memorized incantation. With extreme care blended with haste, he worked on sealing the entire wall so he could get to Grace and talk with her. She was another piece he needed to put firmly in place, and this was the final move. Once she was there, the puzzle would be mostly together, and the rest of his assignment would be easy to complete.

"And now I just have to keep watering these things and watch them grow."

Chapter ④ ⑤

A NEW START

The recent past

"Would you be willing to change rooms with me?"

Devon looked at Arya and moved one of the headphone muffs away from his ear. "What?"

"I wanted to know if you would be willing to change rooms with me."

Devon spun his gaming chair to face his sister. He put the game controller down, tilted his head, and said, "Are you being serious?"

"You know I am."

"Why?"

She shrugged. "I think my energy is wrong for that room. I think it's worth me testing that theory."

"So you want me to sleep in that room thinking it'll make a difference?" He laughed. "You've been insisting for a long time that room is haunted."

"It might be. But you're the hardened skeptic, so what does it matter?"

"I don't suppose it does. Maybe if something happens, it would change my mind."

"So what do you say?"

Devon pursed his lips and rolled his eyes. "Come on, you're being ridiculous. That's a lot of work."

"You scared? Are your hands soft?"

"You're a loser."

"Wow," Arya said, grabbing the door frame. "Tell me you're scared without telling me you're scared. Leaving your sister alone to face whatever has been there for the past however many years makes you a coward."

"You're actually taunting me." He shook his head. "What, are we three years old again?"

"Maybe." She leaned against the wall. "So what's the big deal? You don't believe me and you don't believe in ghosts. I do and I say I've seen and heard them. I'm just saying, if I thought something would help you, I'd do it. And you're supposed to be the guy."

"You're unrelenting," Devon said. He looked at his on-screen character in the video game he was playing just as it was getting executed. "Let's say we do this. What will we tell Mom?"

"That we decided to switch rooms," she said. "We did it to get a change of scenery. Besides, look at how full your room looks. The one I'm in is much bigger. That, right there, is another reason."

"She's going to ask questions."

"I really don't care," she said with a shrug. "We're adults, Devon. If we want to switch rooms, we switch rooms. What does it matter?"

"Alright. I said what I had to say. If it starts something, don't say I didn't warn you. When do you want to do it?"

"Well, we've already eaten dinner and Mom's at work, so why not tonight?"

"That's a lot to do on a school night. I've got a morning class."

"So staying up until one in the morning playing games is OK? You play games every waking chance. It might do you some good to get away from it for a while."

"OK, Mom."

Arya smiled deviously. "What do you say?"

"OK, let's do it."

Arya sat on her bed and gave her new room a once-over. Her anxiety seemed to have already disappeared. Maybe it was the excitement of the moment or that she felt actual relief that she had survived those encounters. Either way, the atmosphere in this room felt completely different in comparison to the other one. There was no denying that.

She walked to her old room and knocked on the door. Devon opened it.

"Hey." She looked inside and saw he'd gotten a lot more done than she was expecting. "It's coming along," she said.

"Yeah," he said, looking over his shoulder. "I just got done hanging the posters. I've still gotta put some stuff away and was thinking I could make some use out of that big closet." He looked at her. "I like it in this room, but my orientation is off. I'm used to being down the hall. How does your new room feel?"

"It feels good. Thanks for doing this."

"Like you said, you'd do it for me." He turned on his computer. "I'm going to get a few games in before going to bed. I'll finish the rest tomorrow. Do you want me to wake you up before I leave?"

"I should be up," she said, then started to walk away. "I have an early shift tomorrow. I'll see you in the morning."

"Arya," Devon said, his tone distressed. She sat up and saw him standing in the doorway, his eyes wide and skin glistening with sweat.

"What is it?" she said, sitting up, fighting the grogginess, trying to understand what was happening.

"There was a sound. It was like scratching or something."

"Calm down," she said. She got up and walked to him. "What are you saying?"

"I heard scratching. I think it was scratching." He pointed at the room. "Then something came climbing out of my poster and was reaching for me."

"What?"

"It sounds crazy," he said, his eyes wide, his lips quivering. "But that's what I saw." He sat down where he stood.

Arya hesitated as a sense of relief consumed her. Maybe it wasn't her this entire time. Somehow, the environment within that room could control anyone's feelings and inspire reactions.

She sat next to her brother. "Hey?"

He looked at her. "I'm sorry."

"For what?" she asked, rubbing his arm.

"Not believing you." He closed his eyes and let his head fall back. "I thought you were crazy. But you're not."

Arya laughed and her hand quickly covered her mouth. "I'm sorry. I'm not laughing at you. It's just redeeming."

"I'm not sure what to make of whatever happened in there. Can I stay here with you tonight?"

"Of course," Arya said, then stood. "I'll get your pillow and blanket."

"No," Devon said. "Don't go in there. I don't like what I saw. Let's leave it in there."

"What else did you see?"

"I don't want to talk about it right now."

"OK," Arya said. "I understand. You can sleep at the bottom of my bed. Try not to kick me."

Devon laughed. "I'll try." He leaned into the hallway and looked at the closed door of his new room. He looked back at his sister. "You're strong, Arya. I want you to know that."

She smiled. "Thank you, Devon."

"I mean it. That was the most frightening thing I've ever seen. I don't think I'll ever be able to forget that."

Chapter ①⑥

DREAM TEAM

The past

"Please come in," Grace said, holding the door for Clyde.

"Thank you," he said, kicking off his shoes as he entered. "I know I'm not the cleanest right now, and I am sorry for not looking presentable. I just got off from working on the auditorium and needed to talk to you about something. Do you have a minute?"

"Yes, of course. Come sit down. Can I get you something to drink?"

"That would be nice."

"Coming right up."

Grace whisked away and soon returned with a glass for Clyde. "Kentucky Bourbon by way of the Mississippi River."

"Appreciated," Clyde said as he raised the glass. "Here's to a lasting friendship."

"I'll drink to that," Grace said, sitting beside Clyde with a Kentucky Bourbon of her own in hand. "So Clyde, what brings you by in such a hastened manner?"

"I wish I could say the visit was for pleasure. But it is not. Although I thoroughly enjoy your company, tonight I've come here to discuss business."

"Business?"

"I am here because I'd like to invite you on the job with me."

Grace smiled. "I'm flattered, Clyde. But that is hardly a place for a lady."

"Well, I disagree." He took a drink. "Please understand that this is all approved by George. I tell you this because he feels the same way. As you well know, George hasn't been feeling well. In an effort to ease his workload and allow him some time to concentrate on his health, I'll be heading up the building projects. I'm hoping you will come on board as my assistant."

Grace crossed her legs and neatened her gown. "Oh, Clyde, I am thankful you've thought of me, but I don't know a thing about construction. Perhaps my efforts would be better served elsewhere."

"Like where?"

"I don't know," she said, contemplating. "Accounting maybe? I'm quite good with numbers."

"I have no doubt you are," Clyde said. "I think you'd be good at anything you put your mind to. But that job will remain in George's custody. It's not laborious, and it will give him something to do while he concentrates on getting better."

"Oh."

"I believe you're the right person to assist me in my efforts. I can think of no one else. What you would need to know, I would teach you. What I really need you for is your organizational skills. You have a sharp mind and pay great attention to detail. I really hope you can see what I see. Anyway, what do you say? Do you want to work with me?"

A smile flashed across Grace's face, and she turned away in an attempt to hide it. "I'm not clear what the details of the job are."

"I would like you to buy the needed materials based on the plans."

"You want me to be a project manager?"

He nodded. "One of the most important jobs. It keeps the wheel turning." He placed his drink down and turned his body so he was facing her. "Now that we're putting the finishing touches on the auditorium, we're getting ready to start George's house. Soon after that, we'll start construction on the hotel. It's going to be a massive undertaking. I could really use your help."

"OK," Grace said, her response more like a thought than an answer.

"OK, what?" Clyde said. "Don't keep me in suspense. I hope that means you are considering my request."

"I . . ."

"You what?" Clyde asked, taking her hand. "I think this would be a wonderful thing for both of us."

"You have the right to know," she said, then sucked in a deep breath. "I have something I need to admit to you."

Clyde sat back, took his glass, and sipped his bourbon, trying not to look desperate. This was an important moment.

"Last night when I was working with my spirit-guide, she told me an offer was coming my way and that it was coming from you."

Clyde nodded and leaned forward, resting his elbows on his knees. "And I consulted mine last night as well."

"And what did he say?"

"That you and I share a bond beyond the physical realm, that our souls are familiar. That I should work on your spiritual growth as much as I work on my own. That your growth within the spiritual camp is as important as anyone's. I was told you would impress upon a lot of people in your time here."

"Wow."

"How about yours?"

"I wish my interaction was as profound as yours, Clyde, but it wasn't. She told me that I was going to have an amazing opportunity coming from you and that I should take it. Imagine my surprise when you showed up at my door with an offer."

Clyde smiled. "It sounds like we have smart guides."

Grace raised a glass, and Clyde met her gesture with his glass. They each took a sip, and Grace said, "I think working together and getting to know each other better will be amazing. It's an opportunity I won't let pass me by."

"This is amazing! To us," Clyde said as he raised his glass again.

"To us," Grace said, clinking her glass against his before they drank and smiled and laughed.

Chapter 07

DISCOVERY

The recent past

"Do you want to explain this to me?" Devon said from the doorway of Arya's new bedroom. His eyes were as wide as the night before, and his face was twisted by anger instead of fear. He dropped a Ouija board at her feet.

She looked at the board before her eyes slowly rose to meet his gaze. Her face paled. "Where did you get that?"

"I was putting the rest of my stuff away and found it on the top shelf of the closet," Devon said, his jaw tight and his fists clenched. "I guess you forgot about it."

"I did because I've never used it."

"Yeah, sure," Devon said, unconvinced. "Is this why I had the experience last night? Have you been using that thing, opening up God knows what and then claiming you don't know what's happening?"

"Devon, I've never messed with it."

"You know what makes it worse? You work on my sympathy bone and get me to change rooms with you. You do this knowing you're putting me in danger so you can escape whatever the hell you created in that room."

"You're back to not believing me?" She turned away and threw herself onto her bed with all of her frustration. "We can change the rooms back if you don't believe me. I would never do anything to put you in danger."

"Why is it in there, Arya? It shouldn't even be in the house."

"Yeah, I know." She bowed her head, her elbows on her knees. "Yes, I thought about using it. I won't insult your intelligence and tell you otherwise. I wanted to contact whatever I was seeing and hopefully understand it. The things that were happening were fine at first, but as time went on, what I saw became more sinister." Her hands wrestled with each other. "The dreams came more often and more vividly. That's when I put the board away for good. I didn't want to make things worse. I had that fear and that's why I never used it."

"Damn, Arya," Devon said, the tension subsiding some. Was she telling the truth or not? Would it even make a difference? She knew better, especially because of all the things she claimed were happening. "Why would you invite things like that into our house?"

"I was desperate for answers," Arya said. "Mom doesn't talk to me because she thinks there's something wrong with me, and you don't ever believe me. What do you expect?"

"For you not to bring something like that inside the house. At the very least, you need to get rid of it."

"I don't disagree. I will."

"Please don't ever do that again, Arya," he said, then turned and walked away.

Chapter ④⑧

A CONFRONTATION

The recent past

"What do you think you're doing?" Jessica, Devon and Arya's mother, said. She was talking to Devon, who had just got home from a full day of college courses.

He looked over his shoulder, half expecting to find someone standing behind him. When he discovered no one was there, he looked at his mother, perplexed. "What do you mean?"

"I don't have time for this, Devon. I was able to pick up an extra shift and I'm getting ready. I've gotta leave in less than an hour."

"I don't know what you're talking about, Mom," Devon said, moving closer to his mother. She always had a certain look when she was pissed off, and boy was she mad. She stood in the hallway, almost dead center between Arya's room and his.

"You're telling me you weren't in that room—which apparently is your room now—dressed in black, wearing a cowboy hat?"

He shook his head. "No." He pointed toward the front door. "I literally just got home."

Jessica looked into the room and then back at Devon. "Something really strange happened. By the way, what is your stuff doing in Arya's room?"

"We switched rooms about a week ago. We wanted a change of scenery."

Jessica watched Devon, her eyes squinting as he spoke. "Uh huh. And whose idea was it to switch rooms?"

Devon hesitated. "It was both of our ideas."

"I don't think you're telling me the truth." She looked in Arya's room. "I'll ask her as soon as she walks in that door. She's due home any minute. If you're lying to me, you're screwed. I don't charge you rent while you're finishing college. If I catch you in a lie, all deals are off. Here's your one and only chance to change your answer. Whose idea was it to change rooms?"

"It was hers, alright?" Devon said, her persistence equally as annoying as the accuracy of her bullshit meter.

"Don't get mixed up in the things she does," Jessica said. "I hope you know better. Your sister thinks she's being sneaky and that I don't know what she's doing. I assure you that I know. This is my house, and I won't tolerate it."

"I don't understand where this is coming from," Arya said. She had just come home from a long, stressful day at work and was ambushed by her mother. If there was anything good about it, it was at least that Devon finally got to see it.

"I was getting ready for work and I saw a person in the hallway walk into what's now your old room," Jessica said to Arya. "He was wearing a cowboy hat or something."

"OK," Arya said. Her confusion forced her eyes to her brother, and then back to her mother. "What does that have to do with me?"

"No, Arya, it's not OK, and we all know it has everything to do with you." Jessica was gathering her things, the tone of her voice vicious. She took possession of her keys, pocketbook, phone, and prepared meals. "Acting like you're confused is infuriating."

"Are you going to work early?" Arya asked.

"I want you to concentrate on what I'm telling you. This conversation is far from over."

"I'm listening, Mom, but whatever happened, I don't know what you think it has to do with me."

"I've tried to ignore it, but it seems you're exactly like your father and nothing like me," Jessica said, then heaved a sigh.

"What are you talking about?"

"I hate to say this out loud, but like him, it seems you're susceptible to the supernatural."

"Wait, you're telling me Dad was a sensitive—or whatever the hell you want to call it—that's why you threw him out?"

Jessica's eyes filled with fury. "You don't get to use that language with me."

"This has to be some kind of joke. He couldn't help it! *I* can't help it!"

"Lower your voice when you're talking to me. I am your mother. What you don't get to do is yell at me in my own house."

"He probably could've helped me. But instead, you sent him away like . . . like he was some sort of leper."

"You don't understand. I was trying to protect you."

"Everyone keeps saying that to me."

"I was hoping that if I kept him away, it would cure you."

"You think I'm diseased? Do you know I had to deal with that crap, night after night, alone, left to feel like I was going crazy?"

"I told you to watch the way you talk to me. I am your mother and you will treat me with respect."

"Well, you're not a very good one."

"Arya!" Devon said as he wedged himself between his mother and sister.

"You mind your own business, Devon," Arya said, stepping past him.

"This is his business," Jessica said. "He lives here, too."

Arya looked at her brother. "Did you know that was why Dad left?"

"The reasons are none of your business," Jessica said to Arya, stealing her attention. "That's between me and your dad. It was best for both of you and our marriage."

"For better with you," Arya barked. "Toss aside the worst. Screw him and screw me."

"Who do you think you are?"

"You put me on medication and cast me aside, and I'm supposed to be thankful?" Arya said, the bite in her voice superseding her mother's. "You stole years of my childhood away from me. You knew what I was going through and you tried to medicate it out of me."

"That is the work of the devil and that is forbidden in my house."

"Do you think I asked for this?"

"He told me he could see and speak to the dead. That is unnatural. He must have done something to earn that. There is no other explanation."

"And what did I do to earn it, Mother?"

Jessica rolled her eyes. "How am I supposed to know? It's not my place to question the reasons things are the way they are."

Arya looked at her brother. "I'm glad you got to see this." She looked at her mother. "You're such a copout."

"Arya," Devon said, his voice high-pitched with the rising tension.

"Stay out of it, Devon," Arya said. "You should just be listening and learning."

"Maybe you're paying the price for the sins of your father," Jessica said with a wicked smile.

"Are you listening to yourself? You're deranged. I mean that sincerely."

"Now you know why I told him to leave. Are you happy? And now I know that you've been spending your time conjuring spirits or whatever they are."

"I didn't conjure anything!"

"Your yelling doesn't convince me." Jessica walked to the front door. "You're old enough now and you have your own source of income. Congratulations. You've followed in your father's footsteps. I want you out of my house."

"You can't be serious!" Arya said.

"Mom!" Devon said.

Jessica twisted the knob and opened the door. "What's going on here and now is long overdue. When you find your place, you can take whatever was roaming around in that room with you." She exited the house and looked back inside. "You have two weeks." Then she slammed the door.

"I didn't say anything to her," Devon said. "I swear it."

"This happens right after you tell me you're going to tell her about my dreams again, and then you find the Ouija board. I'm not stupid, Devon."

"Arya, I swear, I didn't say anything to her."

"And I'm just supposed to take your word for it? Should I do it the same way you did for me?"

"You don't have to take it out on me," Devon said.

"See how that feels?" Arya said. "I'll get my stuff together and find a place. I'm better off."

"Just give her a few days. She'll cool off."

Arya shook her head emphatically. "You heard her—she wants me out. She thinks I'm tainted. I told you I remind her of Dad, and now you know why."

"Yeah," Devon said. "I never knew why he left."

"I tried to tell you and you never wanted to hear it."

"I'm sorry."

"Yeah, I'm sure you are."

"I guess I was afraid that something like this would happen."

"See what ignoring something does? I'm glad it happened."

"You're just saying that."

"No, I'm not. What she did to Dad . . . I'll never forgive her."

"Yeah," Devon whispered. "That's pretty hard to accept."

"I want you to know that you had one experience, and somehow that became my fault. And the person who's supposed to protect me turned against me. That person is you, Devon. I told you never to cross me again, but you did it anyway."

"No, I didn't."

"Yeah, well, I think you did. Now look what happened."

"Arya, please," Devon said, moving to hug her.

"Don't!" she said, pulling away. "Just don't. This is partly your fault."

"My fault!?" Devon said, pointing at himself. "How are you turning this on me?"

"You should've at least pretended to believe me and stuck up for me, Devon. Instead, you sided with her without a thought of what it would do to me, let alone what she did to Dad." She headed to her room. "I've gotta start packing. At least you'll be getting your room back."

Present day

"I think we should go to the chair with a metal detector," Arya said.

"OK," Mila said.

"Like now," Arya said.

"Wait. Like, right-this-second now, or in, like, tomorrow now?" Mila said.

"If we leave now, we should have plenty of time to get there and look. I don't think we should wait."

"Hang on," Devon said. "What's bringing this on? We haven't finished going over the evidence yet. I think we should finish that first."

"There are two words the ITC spit out that keep replaying in my mind," Arya said. "Metal. Dig. It's a simple clue, and honestly, it's going to drive me crazy until we follow up with it. Besides, it's low-hanging fruit. I think we really need to give the area a quick sweep and see what we find."

"Makes sense. I'm in," Mila said, standing and gathering her things. "Bathroom for everyone before we hit the road."

"Hold on a second," Devon said. "I have to be somewhere at six o'clock. Don't I get a say?"

"No, and that's plenty of time for us to look around," Mila said.

"We'll take separate cars just in case we get a hit and it requires more time than you've got. That way you can take off to wherever you're going."

"Alright," Devon said. "Let's get going."

Chapter 09

SOIL AND SPADE

Present day

Arya was on her knees, digging into the packed dirt with a spade. She paused for a moment to catch her breath and to give her tired arms a rest.

"Let me check," Devon said, waving the metal detector over the shallow hole. The machine beeped and Devon pointed to a specific spot. "I don't know how far down, but you're right over it. Dig here."

"I'm having so much fun," Arya said as she wiped her brow, her hands stained with soil. It seemed hotter than usual. She was unsure if it felt that way because of her adrenaline and her desperate need to find what was buried in the earth, or if she was exerting herself and now listening to her body. "Just give me one second." Well, until now. She flexed her hands. "The dirt is really packed."

"Why don't you take a break from digging and I'll do it," Devon said. "Mila can work the metal detector."

"No," Arya barked, and Devon looked at her in surprise. "I want to do it. I have to do it."

"Take it easy," Devon said, backing up a step. "You don't need to yell. You can do it if you want to. You look like you're struggling and I'm just trying to give you a break."

"I'm sorry," Arya said, wiping her mouth with the back of her hand. "I'm just excited."

"I hate to say it, but it sounds more like you're possessed or something."

"You don't need to harp on stuff, Devon. I said I was sorry."

Mila knelt beside Arya and placed a hand on her back. "Are you alright?"

"Yeah. I need to do it. That's all," Arya said as she tried to blink away the sweat in her eyes. "I know you don't understand why, but it's something I have to do."

"The dream?"

"No." She shook her head. "I don't know. It's a strong desire."

"Fair enough," Mila said. "We'll stay right next to you in case you need us. For the record, we feel weird watching you work like that instead of us helping." She sat cross-legged.

"I get it." Arya leaned forward and kissed her cheek. "You're my best friend. Thank you." Without further pause, she worked the soil with the tip of the hand shovel. As she got farther down, the soil quickly changed from a dark brown to a denser brownish yellow.

"I can see from here how hard that is," Devon said. "The good news is that if whatever you're looking for is in that clay layer, it will probably be preserved really well."

Arya kept working until she hit something hard. She looked at Devon and he turned on the detector and put it over the object. The machine squealed.

"Whatever that is, it's steel."

Arya's fingers clawed at the packed clay and muck stuck to the foreign object. She tried to identify an angle or something jutting out so she could grab it and yank it from its resting spot.

"Can I say something?" Devon asked.

Arya continued to work.

"Arya?"

"Hmm?" She paused in her desperation to understand what they had come across. Her face was beet red, her hair sticking to her skin.

"You will need to dig around whatever it is. You won't be able to just pull it out of the ground. All the stuff around it is acting as an adhesive and creating suction."

Arya nodded. "OK."

"A bodybuilder wouldn't be able to pull that out of there."

Arya took control of the spade again and resumed digging, working feverishly to dislodge the metal thing. Sweat dripped from the end of her nose and her face radiated so much heat, she could feel it pulsing outward with every beat of her heart.

After fifteen minutes without pause, Arya had the item more than halfway uncovered. "I can't do it anymore," she said, flexing her hands. A large blister began to form on her palm. "Can you see if you can get it out of there?"

Devon reached into the hole, gripped the metal thing, and worked to release the hold the clay had on it. He stood up and stomped on it.

"Ooh, I think you just broke it free," Arya said, reaching into the hole and picking up the caked steel clump. She twirled it in her hand, trying to figure out what it was. "Well, whatever it is, it's really heavy."

"What is it?" Mila asked, craning her neck to see.

Devon held out his hand. "Can I see it?"

Arya stared at the clump of whatever and handed it to Devon with a shrug. "Have at it."

"Wow," he said, acknowledging the weight by bobbing his hand up and down. He placed it on the grass and dug through his supply pack and took out a bottle of water. He dumped it on the object and the dirt and clay began to fall away.

"Well, what is it?"

"A giant hammerhead?" Devon said, twirling it in his hand to inspect it. "I think it might be a sledgehammer head. I'm not sure what this tapered end is used for, but look at this hole. I think it's where the handle was located."

Arya could see the snapped piece of wood wedged into the oval hole. It had to be petrified.

"Do you know what this might've been used for?"

Devon shrugged. "I'm not very handy, you know that. I'm more of a gadget kind of guy, but we can do some homework and see what we can learn about it. Let's cover this hole back up and get out of here. I've got to head out and want to make sure you guys get out of here OK."

Chapter 20

DISCLOSURE

The past

"Please come inside," George said and moved aside, allowing room for Clyde and Grace to enter his residence. He closed the door behind them. "Can I get either of you anything to drink?"

"No, thank you," Grace said as she sat at the table where flickering candlelight swayed like ritualistic dancers. She took out a folded fan, opened it, and waved it at her face dotted with beads of sweat.

"It is uncomfortably hot this evening, wouldn't you say?" George said, and both Clyde and Grace nodded in agreement. "I've been spending most of my day in the shade, unable to do much of anything physical. I'm finding using the bathroom to be a bit of a chore. I was hoping as the sun set, we would all catch a break from the heat."

"There's not much we can do about the heat," Clyde said. "But there is something we can help with. We wanted you to know that we will handle the laborious tasks while you tend to the other, as per our discussion and agreement, less physical matters."

"Oh?" George said with a growing smile. His eyes bounced between Clyde and Grace. "Is it settled then? You two already spoke?"

Grace nodded and Clyde presented Grace with a wave of his hand. "She is as eager and excited as I am. But I don't want to speak for her, so, Grace, if you would?"

"And I shall," Grace said as she stood and walked to George, stopping in front of him. "Thank you, George. I am excited to learn, and feel honored to help see your vision through."

93

"I am humbled by your love," George said. "From the bottom of my heart, I want to thank you, Grace. But Clyde is the one who deserves the credit. He's the one who suggested you. Although I'm sure you already recognize this, I wanted you to know he has great admiration for your skills."

Grace attempted to hide her smile but failed miserably. "I have become fond of both of you."

"And we of you," Clyde said.

"I agree," George said. "And now that is settled, we shall move at a rapid pace but not so fast that the quality of our plans is compromised. Methodical yet with haste. Does that make any kind of sense?"

Grace and Clyde nodded their agreement.

"I would like to share with you both something private but important to our plight," George said. "A true inside look, if you would entertain me?"

"Of course," Grace said.

"We are honored by your trust," Clyde said.

"As I am by yours," George said. "Can you both be here at first light? It's far too dark out to go anywhere tonight, and I feel I need to organize my thoughts appropriately. I won't hide the fact that I'm feeling worn down. I have a pain in my chest and I coughed blood earlier today."

"Of course," Clyde said.

"Blood?" Grace said, her face showing her shock. "Thank you for telling us. It's important you get rest."

"Thank you and I will," George said. "I am glad for this moment and the optimistic outlook it brings to the future of our camp. It has been a long day. I am sure you are both tired as I am and wish to get some sleep."

Grace and Clyde walked to the door and George opened it for them. "Please, Clyde, make sure Grace gets back to her quarters safely."

"I will make sure she is cared for," Clyde said before walking with Grace into the night.

"That seemed concerningly abrupt," Clyde said. "I'm not walking away with a good feeling."

"I was going to say the same thing."

"I can't help but think how that whole interaction was strange and shocking." He lingered in silence, and then said, "What's your sense?"

"I'd rather talk about what my eyes saw," Grace said, and Clyde nodded. "He sounds and looks tired. Exhausted even."

"The rings around his eyes are prominent. Did you happen to notice?"

Grace began to sob, but took a moment to fight it away. "I hate to say it, but it was impossible to miss. At first I thought it was the candlelight interacting with the darkness. Like it was casting weird shadows." She fell into silence, but soon said, "But then I saw the bags beneath his eyes and how dark they were."

"Yeah," Clyde said, solemn. "I'm sorry. This isn't how I wanted the celebration of our working together to go."

"My heart is breaking for him," Grace said, and then she took Clyde's hand. "It's breaking into pieces."

"I think we need to get his house built sooner than later. That is the first time I noticed how oppressive the feeling is inside his living quarters."

"It may help him."

"I think it will."

"Is it OK if we walk in silence for a while? I need to think."

"Of course we can."

Grace stopped walking, Clyde with her. She placed her head on his chest and began to weep. Clyde wrapped his arms around her and held her tight.

George greeted Grace and Clyde with a smile. "I trust that you both rested well?"

Grace nodded, and Clyde said, "I'm almost embarrassed to admit that I slept like a baby. Finishing up the first-floor lath and plaster work wore me out."

"That's a lot of work," George said. "Your work is exceptional. You sold yourself short on your talents."

"Well, I appreciate that," Clyde said, clapping George's shoulder. "I was always told that a man who talks too much does that to cover for his shortcomings. When you show and don't tell, it doesn't take someone long to recognize the level of your skill and commitment."

"Like you did with Miss Grace here," George said, giving her a playful bump.

Clyde beamed. "Exactly."

"You seem to be in better spirits this morning," Grace said.

"I am," George said, and the rings around his eyes weren't so dark. "It's amazing what a full night of sleep can do."

The night had a series of fast-moving, violent thunderstorms. This allowed the week-long oppressive heat to break. Now, in this early morning, the air had a gentle breeze, and the grass was covered in dew.

"Thank you both for getting up so early. I don't want others to know what I'm sharing with you today," George said. "I've put a lot of thought into it and feel it is the right thing to do. I am trusting you with your silence."

He began to walk in the direction of the lake and they followed him, keeping pace. The conversation paused until they reached the water's edge of the native lake.

"I am not proud to tell you both that I've been hiding something," George continued. "Understand that I don't tell you these things for sympathy, but rather, for your understanding that, even in my absence, these things we have begun to do must be seen to completion."

"What is it, George? What have you brought us here to tell us?" Grace asked. Worry pulled her eyes wide, her focus sharp and unrelenting.

"Look at this," George said, pointing at the lake. A heavy fog hovered over the surface of the water, and it rolled in some sort of dance before the rising sun burned it away forever. "There is such beauty in every moment. We just need to open our eyes to see. Beauty is not meant to be complicated. It is there, right in front of us, waiting to be seen. People convolute things. Sometimes willfully, other times ignorantly. Our plight is to remove that."

"George?" Grace pressed. "The way you're talking . . . are you OK?"

"Yes, I am. I will get to the matter of why I asked you here in a moment," George said. "But in this instance, seeing this with the two of you by my side, it needs to be cherished. We are working a lot, focused on the future with a voracious appetite. I hoped our coming here would allow us to enjoy a bit of the present together."

"Colby Lake," Clyde said after a long silence. His eyes fixated on the things George talked about. "My spirit-guide said this lake would be named after you one day."

"I am not cynical enough to want that," George said. "What I want more than anything is for people like us to have a place to exist without judgment and hostility from religious zealots, doubters, and haters. To be left alone with passive acceptance. Live and let live."

Grace held onto the bend of George's arm. "Being here with everyone, seeing this, makes me feel like I belong to something for the first time in my life," she said.

"I've been battling tuberculosis," George said, the words spoken casually. But once those words came out, everything fell completely silent. So much so that it seemed like this confession stunned the wildlife, and Mother Nature, too.

Grace whimpered and George took her hand.

"I'm not trying to be morbid. I just want a commitment from you both that nothing changes. Whether I am here or not." George turned away from the lake and began to walk through a section of woods that hadn't yet been cleared, gently pulling Grace along, Clyde in tow. "I think it best if the community didn't know. I don't want anything delaying or distracting the people. Momentum is on our side and I feel it imperative it stay that way."

"Treatment?" Clyde said from close behind them, pushing branches out of the way as they moved farther into the forest.

"Here." George stopped at a circular pond that was about fifteen feet in circumference. The water was crystal clear and seemingly four to five feet deep.

"A spring?" Clyde said, looking up from his own reflection and into George's eyes.

"Not just a spring," George said. He pulled a flask out of an inside vest pocket and dunked it into the water. It bubbled until it was full, and then he handed it to Grace. "Taste it."

Grace did, and the purity and coolness of the water widened her eyes and took away her sadness. She handed the flask to Clyde, and his reaction was almost identical.

"This is amazing!" Clyde said, and then he drank some more.

"And according to Seneca, it may be a part of the cure I've been searching for. But I wanted to prepare you both, just in case my time is coming to an end."

Chapter 2<del>1</del>

GATHERING INFORMATION

Present day

The elderly hardware store clerk inspected the heavy, soiled, weather-beaten item he held. Mila and Arya stood beside him, their attention wholly on him and whatever it was he was about to say.

"I'm actually quite familiar with this item," he said, looking at Arya over his thick glasses. "This is a great find. Where did you unearth it?"

"I was metal detecting with my brother and my friend here. The detector started going crazy—"

The man chuckled. "I'm sure it did."

"—and we dug it up." Arya looked at his nametag. "We had a heck of a time getting it out of the dirt, Emil. Is it OK if I use your first name?"

"Clay," the clerk said.

"I'm sorry?"

"Clay. It was most likely a few feet down. That's why it is preserved so well. And yes, of course, you can use my first name."

"What do you think it is?"

"Well, I know for sure it's a straight peen sledgehammer head. It's pretty old. Late 1800 to early 1900 I'm guessing." He angled the item so Arya could see what he was pointing at. "See this area here?"

Arya nodded, already knowing what he was going to say. He was pointing at the oval cutout where a small piece of splintered wood remained.

"This is where the long handle went so they could swing this."

"And what would it be used for?"

"Breaking," the man said. He raised a brow. "Maybe hammering and forming other metal objects such as knives and swords. It had a lot of uses. In fact, this tool is still used today."

"Did they use it for railroad spikes?" Mila asked.

Emil shook his head. "Most likely not. They'd use a tool called a spike maul for that."

"So much for that," Mila said.

"This is all great information," Arya said. "We really appreciate it."

Emil continued to inspect the chunk of metal. "Are you interested in cleaning this up better than this?"

"Is that possible?" She took the hammer head back from him and placed it in a bag. It had a fair amount of weight to it.

"Oh yes, of course," he said and began to walk. For an older man, maybe in his mid-seventies, he got around pretty good minus the hint of a slight limp. "Come with me. That should clean up nicely."

The man stopped at cleaning supplies and handed her something called Ospho, a wire brush, and a disposable paintbrush. "Wash that head off with soap and water, and use the wire brush to help get the crud off. After it dries, use the Ospho here and paint it on generously. That'll help with the rust."

"Wow, that's awesome. Thank you."

"You're welcome." Emil walked to a rack on the side wall. "One last thing." He selected a long, wooden sledgehammer handle and handed it to her. "If you really want to bring that thing back to life, this is the handle to make the sledge usable again."

Arya lit up.

"I told you coming here would be worth it," Mila said. "If we put that handle on, it'll turn this thing into the perfect trigger object."

"Thank you so much, Emil," Arya said. "We really appreciate your help."

"You're welcome," he said. He gave Arya a smile and moved on to the next customer. Arya and Mila hurried to the register with their items.

"I don't know why, but you seem to attract older men," Mila said.

"You're gross. He's just being nice."

"OK," Mila said, shrugging. "I don't know—it looked like flirting to me."

"Give it a rest, would you?"

"Two words."

"Don't you dare."

"Banana," Mila said, smiling. "Hammock."

Chapter 22

PITCH PINE

The past

Grace quickly dressed, then hurried from her living quarters and went outside. Her hair was a mess but she didn't care. She broke out into a run, heading to George's living quarters where she banged on his door with more force than necessary.

"Come on," Grace said, pacing, and then hit the side of her fist against the door again. Every second felt like an eternity. What was taking him so long? Her mind raced with the possibilities of whether or not something bad had happened to her mentor.

Moments later, George opened the door. His tired, heavy eyes looked back at her. He made no attempt to hide his confusion and concern. "Grace? Is everything OK?"

"More than OK," Grace said, pushing her way inside. She rushed to the table and sat. A layer of sweat coated her forehead and she panted from the run and excitement.

"You have me concerned," George said, sitting next to Grace. His unblinking eyes trained on her, his worry seemingly placing him in a temperament of indecision.

Grace shook her head. "This is nothing to be concerned about, Mr. Colby. I promise you that. In fact, I think it's quite the opposite. I was meditating and my spirit-guide came to me wanting to talk about you and your ailment."

"About me?" George said as he rested his elbows on the table. He seemed short of breath and used a hand to prop up his head.

"Yes, about you."

George nodded, his under eyes puffy, the dark rings returning with a vengeance. "Please excuse my lack of excitement. It has nothing to do with you or the purpose of your arrival. I'm still not feeling well."

Grace grabbed George's forearm. "We can see that, and that is what compelled me to seek guidance."

"I think I am in mortal peril, Grace," George said, his eyes unwilling to meet hers.

"The spring—"

"Drinking from it every day," he said.

"I think there is something missing. You need to mix it with pitch pine. That's what my guide told me, and after she delivered the message, she woke me up. As soon as she did, I came over."

"Pitch pine and spring water?"

"Yes," Grace said. "Zippora insisted this would aid you in overcoming this. She said that you should also inhale pine smoke. That combination will help you rid yourself of this ailment."

George nodded his understanding. "I'm willing to try anything," he said. "I'm getting weaker by the day. It now feels like this disease has a firm hold over me. No amount of denial will change that."

"And that is why we have to act immediately," she said. "I'll be back in a little while with everything you'll need to get started. I'll help you with this until you are better. You need to get better, George. You have a lot more to do here."

"Thank you," George said as he moved to his cot. "I don't want to be rude, but if you could help yourself in and out, that would be most helpful. I'm awfully tired and feeling short of breath."

He coughed heavily as he settled onto his cot.

"Have you spoken to your guides?"

"I'm afraid I haven't in quite some time," George said. "I haven't the energy and I don't think they want to risk draining me any further."

Clyde sat on the edge of his cot, his head down and elbows resting on his knees. He had extinguished the candlelight more than an hour ago, and he was calling forth his guide but couldn't connect.

As time moved forward, his frustration subsided some but the initial confusion remained firmly in place. He needed answers so he could plan his next moves.

He sighed, his hands slapping his thighs as he got up, pacing for some time before he sat again. He needed to be patient. That was what he was told.

"Clyde?"

He looked up, and standing by the window was the shadowy outline of his spirit-guide. "Odious. I've been waiting a long time for you tonight."

"Did you hear whether or not Grace gave George the remedy to restore his health?"

"Yes, she did," Clyde said as stood, his confusion validated. "She came to me while I continued to labor in building this camp, per your instructions, planting the seeds of opposition along the way. I don't understand—why was this done? It is a direct contradiction to what we've been doing."

"I need to verify whether she has come to his aid or not."

"Of course she did. You know that is her way."

"Nursing him with the remedy? Attending to him as if he were a babe?"

"Or treating him as if he were a father or mentor? Yes. You know that. You have someone on the inside. Why not ask her?"

"It's better if we limit contact with her. It minimizes the chances of her being discovered. But this is good. Everything is going according to plan."

"Whose plan? If it's not obvious to you, I am confused and require some clarity."

Odious looked over his shoulder at Clyde. "The sun, clouds, sky, or ocean. What difference does it make?"

"None, I suppose."

"None is the answer then. It is the plan and we need to stick to it," Odious said, returning his gaze to the outdoors. "If everything were to fall apart now, we couldn't instill our influence. This place is and will be the size of a major battleground. If something bad were to happen to him, it might be viewed as a tainted land. and we could be risking everyone packing up and leaving."

"No, we don't want that. But I could lead them," Clyde said, indignant. "I could get them to stay. I could continue to build while I sow the seeds of destruction."

Odious sighed. "Power hungry. That is the weakness of your flesh talking. What you're doing now is more effective and will be longer lasting. Don't you see you have access, trust, and influence? Why would you risk throwing that away? Anything that might send scrutiny your way is something to be avoided at all costs."

Clyde watched his guide in the form of a shadow pacing, his hands clasped behind his back and his head down.

"I suppose you're right," Clyde submitted. "That is something I haven't considered."

"George is integral to establishing what we have planned for so long. We cannot, under any circumstances, risk or deviate from what is working and what has been set in motion. I hope you can calm yourself enough to see what I am saying is true."

Clyde sat again. "I saw everything you were saying to be true and right before you completed speaking your sentence. I suppose I just needed to hear it. Even the most trusting heart needs reassurance once in a while."

"That is not your fault, rather, it is the fault of the flesh," Odious said. "If you didn't walk around in that skin jacket, you may be faultless. Now that your heart and mind have been reassured, tell me, have you been carrying on? What else have you accomplished since last we spoke?"

"The walls in the auditorium are done, strategically stuffed with our decree. I'm moving on to George's house while simultaneously working on the hotel." Clyde lay prone, his fingers interlaced behind his head and his eyes clamped shut. "Am I missing anything?"

Odious smiled, and his hand pressed against the window. "Continue to do what you are doing. Build, stuff, and allow your natural human nature to guide you."

"Allow my human nature to guide me? What do you mean by that?" Clyde mumbled, sleep coming fast and hard.

"Give way to the flesh," Odious said, fading into the black. "Be primal and embrace what is to come. You're doing great, Clyde."

Chapter ②③

PIECES TO A PUZZLE

Present day

Arya looked down at herself. Her body lay in a cramped, dark coffin and yet, somehow, she could see things in full detail. The odd thing was she could feel as well as experience the thoughts of both the physical body and of the body she was using to observe.

The inside of the lid was only a few inches above her face. A powerful, musty smell made her nose itch, and she went to scratch it.

"Ouch," she said as her knuckles scraped the coarse underside of the lid and drew blood. Placing her hands on the lid with her palms flat, she pushed with all her might. The thing above her didn't budge, and the impossible weight of it seemed to press down on her even harder now.

The surface felt strangely cold as she allowed her fingers to explore. It was smooth but had portions that were rough, like there was some kind of etching in it. That was most likely where she scraped her knuckles.

Tracing irregularities in the smooth surface, she discovered actual patterns were present. Unsure whether they were letters or diagrams, she moved her hands around only to find more. It was strange how she could see some things, but other things, like the diagrams, were obscured from sight and only discovered by touch.

"What is this thing?" she said, knocking a knuckle against the surface, trying to figure out its makeup. The thumps didn't carry. Dust fell into her eyes and mouth. She broke out in a fitful cough.

"Is this thing I'm inside made out of cement?" she said, trying to bend her legs. The nearness of the concrete slab on top of her stopped her, confined her, controlled her. Whether intentional or not, it created a rising, desperate panic.

"I'm not dead!" she screamed, beating the underside of the lid with her fists. Her flesh ripped, her bones bruised, keeping the outburst to a minimum. She gasped and struggled to catch her breath, her hands falling to her sides. "I'm not—"

Something hard beneath the linens she was lying on caught her attention. This discovery pushed the hysteria away and replaced it with curiosity. Like the carvings, whatever this item was, she couldn't see it. She pulled back layers of fabric, working with minimal mobility but certain determination that, whatever this thing was, it had significance. It was imperative she gain control over it.

Long and narrow, she tried moving it, but whatever it was, the end by her feet had substantial weight to it. How hadn't she noticed this before? Why couldn't she just look down and see what she couldn't observe from inside the casket?

She groaned in frustration.

Whatever made the rules here, the things she was experiencing implied simple logic did not apply. So she had to adjust her approach and control her emotions as best she could.

Working painstakingly slowly to move the object into a position she could identify it in, she quickly realized it was too long to turn in the confined space, so she dragged it up toward her head. Shifting the heavy bottom between her legs, she angled the handle and was able to get it a little closer. Close enough, in fact, that she could reach down and feel the item she now controlled.

It was cold and the handle went into it on one end but didn't extend beyond it.

"Straight peen sledgehammer," she whispered, remembering the item she had unearthed with Devon and the interaction with the hardware clerk.

An idea popped into her mind. A sledgehammer was used for breaking and demolishing things. What she held must've been the key to escaping the compartment she was trapped in. The work needed to achieve that would be strenuous and could take her longer than the amount of air she had left. But she had to try, to chip away at the cement and, hopefully, find her way out.

She angled the hammerhead just so and did her best to use what little room she had to generate as much force as possible, lifting the heavy steel object and smacking it into the cement.

Surprisingly, the cement cracked and splintered as if it were made out of glass. The spiderwebs moved in such a way that Arya could follow them with her eyes. It crackled and soon caved in. Dirt rushed in, pinning Arya down, muting all of her senses as she was covered by the earth in an unstoppable avalanche.

Arya gasped and sat up. Her skin was coated with sweat and her heart pounded something fierce.

"Just a dream," she said into the dark room. She moved to the edge of the bed and wiped sweat off her forehead. "But it might have been more than that."

Chapter 20

DEVIL IN THE DETAIL

The past

"Who is there?" Zippora said as she stood. She had been sitting on the floor, trying to reach Grace. There was much to warn her about, and the situation they were in was dire. Every second counted and this was an unwanted interruption.

"Oh Zippee," a voice sang as the person drew closer, their heels slammed heavily onto the floor, making it obvious they wanted to be known. "Zip–"

"Hello?"

The man stopped singing and walked without saying a word, the footsteps much lighter now. He settled in front of Zippora, clasped his hands behind his back, and rocked on his feet as he stared at her.

Zippora chuckled, looked all around her, and soon settled her focus on the stranger. "What is this? I don't have time for jokes."

"Oh, there is nothing funny about this."

"Umm, OK. What can I do for you?"

"Well," the man said. "You're not going to like the answer to that question."

"And why is that?"

"Because no one likes to be told what to do."

"Then I won't tell you so—I'll ask that you come back some other time. I have a lot of important work to do. I'm sure you do, too. It seems senseless for us to talk when we could be working."

The man shook his head. "I'm afraid I can't do that. Leave, that is. My being here is much more important than your relationship with Grace."

"How do you know Grace?"

"A stone in my shoe, that's how. If you don't stop trying to make that connection with her, only one of us will walk out of this conversation alive."

Zippora chuckled. "You can't be serious."

The man moved even closer. "I couldn't be any more serious if I tried. So what do you say? Will you sever the relationship with her or what?"

"She is mine, and I am hers," Zippora said. "If I were to abandon her, her soul would be ill-fated. Lost."

"Well," the man said. "It is time for you to prepare yourself. I'll only give you a few seconds to do that so the fight is fair."

"Hold on—I'm confused!"

He shook his head. "This is far too pressing for either of us to negotiate. What you claim is yours can never be, just like you trying to buy time by claiming confusion will not work."

"And that is why you've come? To sever or destroy?"

The skin melted off the man, dripping to the floor until the molten flesh hidden underneath was all that remained. "That is exactly why."

"And who is it that I am to battle today? Do I deserve the respect of hearing your name?"

"I am Odious, and I am the essence of turmoil."

"I've heard of you," Zippora said, undergoing a transformation of her own. Her flesh began to glow, beaming light radiating out in an attempt to overcome the darkness that surrounded and consumed Odious.

The two met each other with a violent crash, wrestling for control that didn't work to either's advantage. "I say that because I've destroyed many of your kind," Odious said through clenched teeth. "And this moment will prove to be no different."

"You will come to find that I'll be more difficult to kill than any other before."

"I'll savor it then," Odious said, grunting as he pushed her back. Zippora tried to counter him, but he was too strong. Instead, she moved an arm under his armpit and twisted, using his own momentum and weight against him.

Odious's feet went over his head as he flipped over Zippora's hip. Crashing to the ground with a heavy thud, Odious quickly got up and barreled into her, knocking her down.

"Damn you, vile thing," Zippora said, quickly getting to her feet. "You're as formidable as you claim." She bent the light she controlled, forming it into a sharp sword. Brushing the swathe of hair aside that had fallen into her face, she hunched and gripped the hilt with both hands. "Let's get this over with then, yes?"

Odious smiled with devious intent. "I do things on my terms, and I said I'll savor this fight. That is bad for you."

"Your taunting means nothing to someone like me, who devours darkness. You'll be granted no mercy from me, demon!" Zippora shouted, charging Odious, the sword held ready to strike.

Odious leaped high in the air, twirling, and Zippora ran underneath and past him. He came down gently and shoved her. Falling face down, Zippora rolled to her back and Odious was on top of her, a scythe manifested from shadow held to her neck.

"This is fun, wouldn't you say?" Odious said, smiling. He withdrew his weapon and stepped back. "Go on, get up. Let's do this again."

Zippora struggled to her feet, keeping her eye on Odious as she did so. "This is a game to you?"

"It could've been easily avoided if you'd done as I told you." Odious laughed. "But, it's as I said: No one likes to be told what to do. It seems you're no different, so here we are."

"How does this end?" Zippora asked, circling Odious with her sword at the ready.

He sighed and his shoulders slouched. "With your death, of course. It is vital that you're removed and replaced."

"So it will be an equal application, and I declare this will only end with your death then, demon." She lashed out, swinging the sword over her shoulder and toward his back. In an instant, a dark shield formed from shadow protected Odious's back, easily thwarting the blow.

"I'd prefer an angel but I guess I'll have to settle for a clairvoyant today," Odious said, his face twisted with rage. A spinning backfist connected easily and firmly on Zippora's jaw, knocking her down.

"Get up!" Odious shouted. "Get up and feel my rage!"

Zippora scrambled to her feet, her ears ringing from the blow. She stood at the ready, fighting off the dizziness, trying to slow things down so she might regain her balance. This was her only chance to survive this.

Odious wasn't waiting anymore. It seemed the rage had put him in a frenzy. He created a double-headed hammer out of shadow, massive and heavy. He swung it, his movement telegraphed and easily avoidable for Zippora.

She ducked underneath his sluggish attack, went to a knee, and swiped her sword across his belly. Odious hesitated, stopped, looked at what Zippora was able to do, and dropped his weapon. It disintegrated as he fell to his knees and then to the floor.

"Rahhh!" Zippora screamed and went to deliver the killing blow.

"No, please," Odious begged, rolling to his side. He lifted his hands and looked into Zippora's eyes. "Please, sister, don't hit me anymore."

Zippora hesitated. The once angry demon had been reduced to a sniveling child. His skin was no longer red and threatening.

"Damian?" Zippora said. She lowered her sword and motioned to touch her brother and offer him comfort. This was something she hadn't done in life. Her ignoring what was happening to him tormented her long after he had died. Maybe she could use this moment to make up for what was lost.

"Damian," Zippora whispered, extending a hand to help him up. "I'm so sorry."

"I am too," Odious, presenting himself as Damian, said. He reached up, grabbed Zippora by the back of her neck, and yanked her downward while driving a long, curved, serrated dagger into her gut.

She gasped, looked down at the damage, and then her eyes focused on Odious, who now appeared as himself. "Why?"

"Because you're in my way," Odious said, twisting the dagger. "I believe I told you I would make this fun. I hope I didn't disappoint." He twisted the sharp instrument again. "As I reflect, I believe I did. I want you to understand that because, although it wasn't fun for you, that doesn't mean it wasn't for me."

Odious ground the dagger around, slashing everything inside her gut before she finally fell over in a heap.

"And that is how I got rid of her," Odious said.

Clyde sighed and shook his head. "You couldn't have told me you killed her? Wouldn't that have been easier?"

"I suppose it would have been, yes." Odious chuckled in delight. "But where is the fun in that? We work hard, so why not embellish? Telling things like I did from her point of view was rather exciting for me. I hope you found some joy in it, too."

"Yeah," Clyde said, nodding. "It was interesting enough, I suppose. But to know she's out of the way for good makes me feel a bit more comfortable. Navigating around without her guide posing a threat is game-changing." Clyde raised a brow at Odious. "I didn't know her guide was human."

"She was into the occult, and when she was tinkering, she opened a portal. Her brother became a target of possession and had a seizure and died. She blamed it on her own actions and changed her ways, swearing revenge against those she felt were responsible." Odious clicked his tongue. "It is a shame, really. She would've been a useful and powerful ally."

"Was she right? Did it have anything to do with spirits?"

Odious shrugged. "It doesn't matter. She was an enemy and needed to be treated and dispatched as such. I found what I needed and used it against her. All you need to know is she's dead."

Chapter ②⑤

THE MEANING

Present day

Arya picked the sledgehammer up and settled her dominant hand's grip close to the head, her other hand toward the bottom portion of the newly installed wood handle. The heavy tool felt powerful and destructive in her hands.

"I'm going to smash it," Arya said, her eyes fixed on the concrete and brick chair. She didn't care if anyone was watching her or not.

"What are you talking about?" Mila said. "You can't just smash the chair. We talked about vandals and respecting the graveyard."

Arya fell into deep thought. The headstones, the dry grass underfoot, and the people around her melted away, replaced by her looking down on herself in the coffin. The overwhelming need to break the slab of concrete that sealed her inside the casket surged through her veins.

"Break it," she muttered. "That's the only way. It has to be done."

But something was missing. Her thoughts were racing and she needed to slow them down. Recklessly breaking the chair wouldn't provide her with any answers. There was a reason they'd found the sledgehammer, cleaned it, and replaced the handle. There was a deeper meaning behind that vivid dream that came after and the things she couldn't see. The tool was meant to be used for something. Whatever that something was, she was certain it would bring her that much closer to finding whatever it was she was supposed to be looking for.

"What am I missing?"

"What did you say?" Mila asked. "You're mumbling."

"Nothing," Arya said, remembering how she had to break the slab of cement above her.

She took a step closer to the Devil's Chair, her focus bouncing between her visions and the reality of being in the graveyard with Mila and Devon. They probably thought she'd gone full crazy, but she didn't care. The puzzle she found herself immersed in was far more important than their misguided opinions.

The need to break the slab of cement above her was overwhelming, encouraging her to recklessly swing the sledge to see where it would hit and what it would expose.

"Because," she said, looking up at nothing. But she could feel how close it was to her face. "Because it is a lid. It was the inside part of a covering."

She drew the heavy hammerhead back and, with as much strength as she could muster, she sent it crashing into the side of the Devil's Chair. A single brick broke away, creating a fist-sized hole that released the air long ago sealed away. She could've sworn the air hissed as it escaped, but she wasn't completely sure it wasn't imagined. The whiff of stale air was strong.

"Arya! What did you do?" Mila said, snapping Arya to awareness.

She looked at Mila, returning to the now. She saw the hole, the sledgehammer handle still firmly in her grip, and Devon's concerned gaze looking back at her from behind Mila.

"I don't . . ." Arya backed up a few steps, dragging the heavy hammerhead through the patchy grass. "I don't know why I did that."

"We were calling your name, and you weren't responding! It was like you were in some sort of trance," Mila said. "You scared the crap out of us."

"Hmm," Arya said, assessing the things around her. No matter how she tried to focus on Mila's and Devon's concerns, her attention was drawn to the hole she'd made. It was like she had a mission, and any distraction needed to be ignored—no matter what.

She let go of the hammer, reached into her pocket, and took out her cell phone.

"Arya, what are you doing?" Devon said. "We have to get out of here. The cops are going to come, and if they were to catch us, you'd go to jail for vandalism."

Arya shook her head and turned on her phone screen, accessed the flashlight and then the video recorder.

"No one heard us," she said, her words coated with certainty. "And they're used to visitors coming by in the daytime. If anyone is near, I don't think they're even paying attention to us. I think things beyond our understanding are making sure of that."

"Arya?" Mila said. "What's gotten into you?"

"This is how she would get sometimes when we were kids," Devon said.

"What do we do for her?" Mila asked.

Arya knelt beside the chair and stuck the phone into the hole, blindly moving it around.

"I don't know," Devon said. "I didn't know then and I don't know now."

"The answer is here," Arya said as she sat on the chair. Eagerly flipping through the phone, she played the video.

Mila moved next to Arya and looked at the phone, and soon Devon did too. Tension lingered in the air as the video displayed what it had captured. The camera moved around and focused on the underside of the bench. There, etched into the cement, were writings and strange symbols.

Mila gasped and covered her mouth. "Oh my God."

"That's what she was trying to tell me," Arya said. "This is what that dream meant. She was trying to show me the underside of the seat."

"Who is she?"

"I don't . . . I don't know, but I think it has a connection to the lady on the porch. This is starting to make sense to me."

Chapter 26

SPARK

The past

Clyde knocked on the rickety front door, and by the way it rattled, he contemplated whether or not he had used too much force. For some odd reason he was extremely nervous and couldn't understand why. From the moment he decided that this was where he was going after work, and during the entire journey here, the fluttering in his chest wouldn't let up.

He looked out into the night, searching for a distraction. Turning his eyes to the sky, he couldn't help but acknowledge the beauty of the moon and the stars. George was right. The beauty was all around them. They just had to pay attention and they'd see it. The night sky seemed exceptionally bright tonight and, perhaps, the full moon was the source of his anxiety.

A cool breeze was much appreciated, and he swatted at a mosquito buzzing around his ear. If there was anything he hated about where he was, it was that.

"Clyde?" Grace said, and he stiffened. He hadn't heard her open the door and felt silly having been caught sparring with an insect.

"Hello, Grace," he said, trying to ignore the embarrassment that most likely pulled the color out of his face. He cleared his throat and said, "I hope I'm not interrupting. Are you busy?"

"No, not at all. I'm just relaxing after the long day," she said as she stepped aside. "But not as long as yours, I'm sure. I really wish you would slow down. Come on inside."

He did, and walked to the center of the candlelit room, the heels of his boots beating the wooden planks.

"Would you like something to eat or drink?" Grace said as she closed the door, keeping the crazed bloodsuckers at bay—for now.

"I would really enjoy a drink." He turned and looked at her with a smile. "If you have any of that wonderful whiskey that came via the Mississippi, that would surely hit the spot."

"That's a wonderful suggestion," Grace said, then went into the kitchen area. "And I think I'll join you in that if you don't mind. It has been a long day."

Of course he didn't mind, but he didn't take what she said as a question. "Indeed it has."

"It cooled off nicely tonight. Finally." She poured the drinks. "It appears as though the change of season is upon us. Did you just get off?"

"I did," he said, stretching. The pain in his lower back made him wince. "I've been on my feet all day and bent at odd angles while I was working."

"I can see your discomfort from here." She handed him his drink. "This is the last time I'll say it, but I think you're working too much. Maybe you should take a day off and rest your body."

Clyde stood up straight, tried to will away the ache, and said, "Nonsense. We don't have time for that. We are so close that if you reach your hand out, you can practically touch it."

"Alright. No breaks then. Maybe you should head back to work right now. Those walls won't build themselves," she said with a laugh, then raised her glass. "But we have time for one of these, right?"

"More than one, if you'd like. But I don't ever want to impose."

"You're not imposing. In fact, I'm glad you stopped by. I was struggling to make a decision on what to do."

"I'm glad you feel I can assist you, because it's usually you who is assisting me. How can I help?"

"I thoroughly enjoy your company, Clyde."

He looked away shyly. "And I enjoy yours, too."

They exchanged a smile.

"By the way, we're almost four months ahead of schedule," Grace said.

"And I plan on keeping that lead and expanding it if we can. It's important for a lot of reasons. One being George's well-being. It allows him to concentrate on the healing plan you placed him on." He looked around. "And, like I said to George, your organizational skills have kept us ahead of schedule and kept him on the healing path. You've been invaluable to all of us in so many ways. When he sees the results of what we've accomplished, he won't be able to deny how effective we've been as a team."

"You know I'm not very good with compliments," Grace said.

"I don't mean to make you uncomfortable. I'm just speaking the truth."

"Did you want to sit?" she asked, pointing at a wingback chair.

"Thank you," he said as he determined what was closest.

"Sit here—it should help with your aches," Grace said, pointing at a chair closest to her.

"Thank you," he said, and then sat. He sank into the chair. The curve of the back contoured against him perfectly and kept him upright. He could feel the pain beginning to release its hold. "I might stay right here in this chair tonight. Sorry, boss, I'm not going back to work tonight."

She laughed. "You better not, and you can stay if you'd like."

"I appreciate that, but aside from the great conversations we always have, there's another reason I stopped by tonight."

"We'll get to that in a minute," Grace said, as she placed her glass on the table next to the chair and went behind him. "Just try and relax for a minute." She rubbed his shoulders. "Is this OK?"

Clyde closed his eyes, feeling her strong hands ease the tension. His skin goosed, her touch grew sensual, and it made him acknowledge that she made him nervous. He liked her mannerisms, the way she smelled, laughed, and spoke. Heck, he even liked the way she ate. She was delicate yet strong and had endearing eyes. He began to think of her as much more than a friend. "It is the most wonderful thing ever, thank you."

"I know you've been busy and bogged down with work, but have you had any updates about George?"

"No," he said, his head low, his focus in tune with her touch and her warm breath on his neck. "That's the second reason I stopped by. I didn't hear anything and was wondering what was happening. I didn't want to drop in on him, knowing how bad he's been feeling."

"I think today he's finally taken a turn for the better. The past twenty-four hours has given me encouragement about his progress," Grace said.

"That's wonderful news. I was worried about him."

"I was, too." Grace paused what she was doing. "Everyone was. I'm ashamed to admit I was worried that if the worst had happened to him, the effect it would have on the camp and everyone involved would be catastrophic."

"I've thought that, too," Clyde said, his voice heavy with the burden of such an event coming to pass. "There is no denying he is the glue that holds everything together."

"I think we should go see him before work in the morning. He asks about you all the time. I know he holds you in high regard, and he would absolutely light up seeing you."

"I think that's a great idea." Clyde sat in silence, and Grace began to massage his shoulders and neck again. "Would you like me to stop by in the morning so we can walk together?"

"I would have it no other way," Grace said, the playfulness in her voice palpable. "By the way, Clyde. You said there were two reasons for your coming here tonight, and you've only told me about one."

"That's true, isn't it?"

"I think it is."

Clyde stood, met Grace's gaze as he walked around the back of the chair. He stopped where she stood, heaved a sigh, took her hands into his, and invoked the courage to speak. "I've grown very fond of you, Grace."

She smiled, looked at their clasped hands and then back into his eyes.

"I'm not very good at things like this," he continued. "Please forgive me if my words don't come out quite right."

Grace nodded. Clyde could see that she, too, was nervous.

"I am smitten with you. I would like to be more than friends, if you feel the same way I do."

"Are you talking about courtship?" Grace said, her reply barely above a whisper.

"I would ask your father and mother, but being that's not possible, I didn't know how else to ask."

"You did wonderfully," Grace said.

"I did?"

Grace nodded and her eyes welled up with tears. "You did."

"Wow. OK," Clyde said. He just stood there, holding her hands. "Now it's going to get really awkward. What do we do next?"

Grace laughed, grabbed their drinks, held up her glass, and said, "How about a toast to us?"

"To us," Clyde said. He touched her glass with his and they drank.

Chapter 27

SYMBOL OF CHAOS

Present day

Mila, Arya, and Devon worked feverishly to cast the video from the phone onto the television. They hatched the plan on the way home from the Devil's Chair, and the buzz in the car was that of excitement. Once they got it connected, the picture looked sharp and clear, making the details of what Arya captured much easier to see. They played the video, their focus on the screen and the once-hidden details of what was beneath the seat.

"Wait, pause it there," Devon said. He moved close to the TV and copied one of the symbols onto a piece of paper.

"What is that?" Arya said, turning her head so she could see the carving better.

"I don't know," Devon said. "But I'm going to do my best to figure it out."

"It's amazing how pristine and clear the engravings are," Mila said.

"It's no surprise," Devon said. "Think about it. All this time, the carvings were protected against the elements, keeping them perfectly preserved."

"I wonder who made the chair and who engraved the symbols and for what purpose."

"I don't know, but I'm certain they wanted them intact to make sure they stayed potent."

"That seems logical and serious," Mila said.

121

"Hang on," Devon said, looking at Mila who was controlling the cell phone. "Play it and pause it again. Let's see what else we can make out."

Mila did just that, and from the new angle on the screen, it was easy to see two more etchings, one recognizable by all three and spoken aloud by them, too.

"That's a freaking pentagram."

"And look," Arya said, pointing at the symbols on the TV. "These seem to have been done in some sort of order." She touched the screen while she spoke, guiding Mila and Devon's eyes. "One here, here, here, and although we can't make out what these are, there seems to be at least one more on the slab over here. If I'm not mistaken, when you sit on the seat part of the chair where your butt goes, these symbols are facing or pointing south. Can either of you see that?"

"Wait," Mila said, turning her body to orient herself with the chair. "Which way is the chair facing?"

"Oh yeah," Devon said, his eyes sweeping over the symbols. "Good catch, Arya. It's telling that the etchings are in a row and that they're facing south."

"What's the significance of them facing south?" Mila asked.

"When something faces south, it could very well signify rebellion and most certainly opposition to Christianity," Devon said.

"How do you know these things?" Mila whispered. "And you blurt that out without looking it up."

"We have to get back out there," Arya said. "We have to see what the other symbols are underneath there. I'll bring my selfie stick. I should be able to take better pictures that way."

Devon put up his hands. "Wait a second. Let's slow down here. I put things back so no one would see the hole in the side of the chair. It's not going anywhere, and we have enough here to keep us busy for at least a few days, if not more."

"I agree," Mila said. "We've taken big bites and I think we should chew for a little while."

"Maybe I'll go alone to see what I can gather," Arya said.

"Absolutely not," Devon said. "You're still wanting to run off. I would prefer you didn't do that and that you took a step back to see that something else is trying to influence you."

"He's not wrong," Mila said. "Whatever was happening to you at the chair was a bit scary to watch." Her eyes welled with tears and her voice cracked. "I won't pretend to understand anything about that, but I also won't pretend to act like nothing happened."

Arya hugged Mila. "I'm sorry, I didn't realize how this was affecting you."

"We do this together and we do the best we can to try and keep some order," Devon said.

"I want Mila to understand what it's like because it might help her," Arya said. "I feel restless. It's like I have a strong hankering or an invisible hand trying to push and pull me, encouraging me to be where it wants me to go."

"Can you resist it?" Mila asked.

"Yeah, I think so," she replied, her tone oozing with uncertainty.

"I let you down before, and I don't ever want to do that again," Devon said. "I'm asking you to communicate with us so we can try and protect you. In the meantime, we finish the footage and audio review of the investigation, then we go out there."

Arya held a hand out to Devon. "Can you give me the drawing you made of the symbol so I can investigate that? It'll help distract me from what I really want to do."

Devon handed her the mock-up, and Arya took it, retreating to a chair. She opened her cell phone, took a picture of the image, allowed the image finder to do its work, and then read the results.

"Well, that's concerning," she said, holding her phone up for Devon and Mila to see. She was too far away for them to make out any of the details.

"I can't see it—what does it say?"

"Well this symbol"—she held up Devon's sketch—"is literally called the Symbol of Chaos."

"Are you kidding me?" Mila said, the concern in her voice rising with the question.

"I wish I was, but I'm not."

Chapter ②⑧

THE NEXT STAGE

The past

"I want to thank you for everything you've done for the community," George said. His breath was wheezy and it made him cough often.

"It is my pleasure," Clyde said, sitting next to Grace at his bedside.

"You, young lady, are selfless," George said to Grace. "For your hard work and for your care of me. You have sacrificed a lot."

Grace's eyes settled with tears as she nodded. "Clyde wanted to see you. I thought if you had a visitor, it might help lift your spirits."

"And it has," George said before he gasped for air. "I want you both to know I think you will make a wonderful couple."

"How?" Grace said, and she looked at Clyde to see if he was the one giving it away. Clyde just sat in stunned silence.

"Oh, please," George said, giving in to a coughing fit. "It doesn't take a psychic to see the chemistry and energy swirling between the two of you. It's radiating and is so bright, I practically have to squint when I look at either of you."

"I assure you, we will keep it away from everyone else," Clyde said. "It will be business as usual."

"I don't see the need for that," George said. "I think it's a wonderful thing. I believe the world can use more love. This is something to celebrate, not hide away so others don't see it."

Grace took George by the hand. "Thank you for your blessing."

"Ah," George said, waving his hand. "You don't need my approval. You just need the approval of each other."

Clyde and Grace looked at each other and held hands.

"Grace and I began laying plans for the next phase after the hotel is built. We both agreed that we wanted to move you into your new home as soon as possible," Clyde said. "We are hopeful and believe you are on the mend, but we also believe a change of scenery would do you wonders. Just being in a brighter room will go a long way in building your spirits and repairing your health."

"But the work for the auditorium was just completed and the hotel is only partially built. Won't the construction of the new house take, at the very least, several months to complete?"

"That is what we wanted to share with you. We believe we can have you in the house in a few weeks."

"How is that possible?" George asked, his eyes volleying between Clyde and Grace.

"We propose to frame the house, put up the exterior walls completely, and finish your bedroom and washroom. This will get you into your new house. As time and your health permit, we will finish the rest of the house."

"What do you think?" Grace asked with a smile so big it showed her teeth.

George stood, walked to the table, and sat. "I think the time for robust change is here. This home has served its purpose. I can't say I'll miss it. The new place will be the catalyst to dismantle the temporary shelter, marking it as the beginning stages of getting everyone into their permanent residences."

"This is all so very exciting," Grace said. "We are at the crux of big changes and I can feel it."

"There is more news," Clyde said. He sat at the table with George. "With the progress we've made on the hotel, we can begin focusing more on tourism. We should have the bottom floor completely finished in about five weeks. With your blessing, we would like to start taking reservations. It will keep us focused on meeting a deadline that is"—he looked at Grace, then at George—"that we believe to be easily achievable."

George sat back in the chair, and it creaked under the weight shift. His fingers twirled his mustache as he contemplated things. Then, a satisfied smile took over and his eyes welled with tears. "We're really that close?" he said as he stood. Clyde stood with him and George hugged him. "Yes, of course! Let's let everyone know."

Chapter ㉙

DETAILS

The past

When Zippora looked at the people around her, it was like peering at them through a dirty window. They were among the living, and to them, she would be considered dead. Now wasn't the time to contemplate the details of how these things worked. Somehow, she needed to figure out a way to get their attention, and needed to do it as quickly as possible.

The people moved about, oblivious to her nearness and her need to get their attention. They were busy coming and going, unaware of the evil that lurked around them.

She thought to scream and yell and even attempt to gather enough energy to make physical contact, but she needed to stick with her plan, believing it would work.

When she was attacked by Odious, she was beaten unconscious, dragged somewhere unknown to her, and left with the idea of never being able to escape. Although she was lost within a labyrinth of confusion, she had no doubt that its design was from a devious nature and intended to never be defeated. Knowing that encouraged her more, and she was determined to undo what was done.

Roaming lightless hallways that twisted and turned and led to dead ends, she worked painstakingly slowly to familiarize herself with anything that could be used to identify her whereabouts. Having to double back and try different routes was daunting but not impossible to figure out.

Whether it had been a week, several months, or years that had gone by, she wasn't sure. The maze had succeeded in turning her around early, and the darkness was so deep that it revealed nothing. It succeeded in muting and confusing her senses. But that didn't matter, because she had work to do, and regardless of how she felt, she had to find her way out, so she pressed on.

Then the day came when she simply walked out of the maze and into the light they desperately tried to keep her out of. And now, as she could see the living carrying on with their business, oblivious to her and the evil seeds that had been planted all around them, she tried to figure out a way to reestablish the connection she had with Grace. In order to do so, she had to first rid Grace of the thing that Odious had attached to her.

Certainly, some sort of sorcery bound Grace to whatever was meant to take Zippora's place. She knew Grace was under the influence of the surrogate, and was making decisions she wouldn't have normally made.

In order to break that spell, she would have to destroy it. And as she observed the oblivious people, it only made sense how Odious, with the use of Clyde, was able to accomplish the things they had.

So, she sat on the floor of the newly built hotel and positioned herself where most of the guests and staff would travel, and remained in a dormant state so she could gather as much of their energy as possible.

Day after day she repeated the process, and then went to one of its last unfinished rooms on the upper floor where she would concentrate that energy and manipulate the electrical wiring in the wall.

This process went on for years until, one day, the wire shifted, encouraged by her touch, and it created a spark. The wood inside the walls began to smolder and, soon after, burst into flame. The flames spread quickly and consumed the hotel, burning the incantations placed within the walls and floors and ultimately releasing everyone from that which restricted and manipulated them, including Grace and the spell that was used to attach the fake guide to her.

"Now it's time to execute the final stage of my plan," Zippora said as she watched the hotel burn.

⌁⊶⊙⊷⌁

Present day

Arya sat up. The dreamlike vision was so real, she swore she could touch the energy manipulation and feel the heat of the flames.

Groggy, she grabbed her phone off of the nightstand and opened a search browser. She typed in: *Cassadaga hotel fire.*

The results that came back stunned her.

Construction on the Cassadaga Hotel began in 1894 and was completed in 1901. The hotel burned down in 1926 due to a faulty electrical system.

The hotel was rebuilt in 1927 and reopened in 1928.

Chapter ③⓪

WATER UNDER THE ROCKS

The past

"I now pronounce you husband and wife," the cleric said, and everyone who came to see the marriage between Clyde and Grace stood and applauded.

The couple shared a kiss, then held hands to face the people for the first time as husband and wife.

George stepped forward and gave Grace a hug. He extended a hand to Clyde, and Clyde hugged him instead.

"Congratulations," George said.

Clyde whispered into George's ear, saying, "If you don't mind, I have a few words I need to say."

"Of course," George said. "It is your day." George faced the crowd and held his hands up. "Everyone, Clyde just informed me that he would like to say a few words."

George stepped aside, giving Clyde the floor. Everyone was quiet, their attention on Clyde as he pulled out a piece of paper from his pocket, mopped the sweat off of his brow, and cleared his throat.

"Wow. This is, by far, the happiest day of my life," he said, sharing a warm smile with Grace. "I felt it important to mention, as we chose this day to celebrate our love, the events of my life since I arrived here in Cassadaga over three and a half years ago.

"First, I want to thank George for allowing me to be a part of this community. If it wasn't for him and his vision, I wouldn't . . ." He paused to gather himself. "No, allow me to say this right. We like-minded people wouldn't be here, with a new hotel, homes, a welcome center, and a lending library, if it wasn't for George's vision and ambition.

"Of course because of his acceptance, I eventually met my beautiful wife, Grace, who is and has been an integral part of my life and this wonderful community. She oversaw and coordinated the building of every single structure we have, and helped our founder, George Colby, to defeat tuberculosis. Thanks to her guidance and care, Mr. Colby is all but healed. The only reminder that remains of his illness is the little cough that lingers. The good thing about that is he won't be sneaking up on anyone soon."

Everyone laughed, and although he couldn't have timed it any better if he tried, George coughed.

"Grace is such a strong woman. So with that said, Grace, my wonderful wife, thank you for allowing me into your life and for everything you've done for me and this community."

Clyde folded the paper and put it away. "Well, that's all I have to say. Thank you to everyone who came to celebrate with us. We, as a people, have a lot of reasons to celebrate. After all, we live in the most beautiful place on earth. Water under the rocks!"

Grace stepped forward and motioned to Clyde. "Well," she said to the gathered. "I'm not going to attempt to outdo that. We are thriving because each and every one of you contributed. We all have a lot to be proud of. I know I am." She looked at Clyde and smiled. "Early on when I was getting to know Clyde, I was offering him some advice. After I gave him my opinion about a few things, one of the things I told him was how he needed to work on his Southwestern accent, and if my memory serves me right, that was the first time I called him a cowboy. He didn't lose or work on his accent, and I find it endearing."

George handed Grace a bowler cowboy hat, and she placed it on Clyde's head. "I've always wanted to see him in one of these, and I must say, Mr. Stolly, that you wear it well. You're my cowboy."

Chapter ③④

ACTIVATED

The past

"You need to wake up."

Clyde twitched as he was yanked from his sleep. He struggled to focus his eyes, and when he did, he saw Odious standing in the doorway of his bedroom. He watched Odious walk into the living room, and while he waited for Clyde, he paced. Clyde knew having him just show up at his house unannounced now that he was married couldn't be anything good.

"What is it?" Clyde asked, whispering so he wouldn't wake Grace.

"I don't want you questioning the reasons why, I just need you to do it," Odious said with a severity Clyde hadn't heard before. He stopped pacing and looked Clyde in the eye. "You need to go now. Kill George and then flee."

"Kill George?" Clyde said, confused. Was this was some sort of lucid dream? "You've gone out of your way to keep me from killing him and now you wake me up, and without warning, you order me to kill him?"

"We've been discovered and it no longer matters," Odious said, heaving a sigh. "The community is built and our mark has been left everywhere. Our work is done here."

Clyde looked over his shoulder and into the bedroom where his wife slept. He could see the gentle rise and fall of her chest as she breathed peacefully.

"Give me a break, would you?" Odious said, stealing Clyde's attention. "You don't really love her. I made you think and feel like you did."

"You did what?" Clyde said, finding himself in conflict with his own feelings. What Odious was saying defied what was in his heart.

"I told you we don't have time. Making haste is our only chance of getting out of this unscathed. Especially you."

Clyde sat in disbelief and he watched Odious pace. "I . . ."

"You what?" Odious bit back. "Zippora has returned. I'm sure you know what that means?"

Clyde stood. "Grace's guide? But how?"

"When the hotel burned, it freed her from her confinement."

"But the story you told me. You told me you killed her."

"Yeah, about that," Odious said, then laughed. "I might've embellished a little bit."

"You . . . you lied to me?"

"Oh, get over yourself, Clyde. Seriously, I'm a demon. What did you expect?"

"The truth! That's what I expected. The things I've done and the decisions I've made were based on your guidance and the idea I was being told the truth."

"And the guidance I've given you is and was sound. Tick-tock, Clyde. The window of opportunity is closing rapidly."

"If you lied to me about my feelings for Grace and about destroying her guide, then what else have you lied to me about?"

Odious shrugged. "You're getting bogged down by human concerns. Do you think you really meant those things you said in that speech? Oh, George this and Grace that. Give me a break. I'll tell you what and I'll keep it simple. Grace can live if you do what needs to be done and do it quickly. We have no time left, now go."

Seneca stepped out of the shadows as the drums of war pounded with intensity. Now that the spells had been broken, he could see everything for what it was. This demon would come to know the wrath of a true warrior. There was no time to waste, so he hurried to George.

Chapter ③②

RECONNECTION

The past

"Grace?"

Grace sat up in bed, rubbed her eyes, and stretched. Something felt off. When she looked at the opposite side of the bed, she noticed Clyde was gone. It was pre-dawn and he usually didn't leave until first light.

Maybe she had been tossing and turning too much and he went to the couch. Her day had been long, and falling asleep wasn't something she could resist once her head hit the pillow. Over the past week she noticed her body ached, and at first she thought she was getting sick. But she self-diagnosed, noticing her breasts were exceptionally tender, and with that acknowledgment, she realized her cycle was late, too.

"Grace?"

She froze because she didn't recognize that voice.

"Look within and find the truth."

Those words turned her attention internally, and mentally she stepped to an unseeable edge. When she looked down, the height in which she found herself made her tingle. Instinctively she went to step back, but something behind her forbade it, and shoved her forward.

She fell and tumbled through the air. Instead of fearing the coming impact, she found herself searching for an answer that remained just out of reach. Something else was going on, but she couldn't finger it. She felt different somehow, like the connection she had with her guide had been severed.

She closed her eyes and concentrated. Zippora was there, fighting against the wind as they descended, reaching a hand out. "You need to take my hand, Grace."

Grace did and she stopped descending and began to float like a feather until her feet touched the floor in the bedroom.

"There is no time for you to question what I say. You must act and do so swiftly," Zippora said.

The spirit-guide was radiant but obviously weighed down by grievous earnestness. That prompted a flood of questions to come over Grace, but she resisted asking them, and instead trusted in her guide. "OK."

"Clyde is not who he says he is, and the guide you thought was me, wasn't. I need you to look in his dresser and find the pages adhered to the underside of the bottom drawer."

Grace moved to Clyde's dresser, got on her hands and knees, and looked where Zippora instructed her.

"You, George, and the rest of the members of the camp are in terrible danger from him and the things he's done around the community."

Grace pulled the pages out from their hiding place, and she looked at them, stunned.

"I'm sorry, but you must blindly trust in me and move with an urgency you've never had before," Zippora said. "Time is of the essence."

Grace took the papers to the foot of the bed and spread them out. On each page were symbols she wasn't familiar with, but next to each symbol, Clyde had made a note. The things it said were confusing and equally concerning.

The symbol of chaos, said to represent concepts like balance, harmony, union, and the interconnectedness of opposing forces. Another, which looked like a circled upside-down star, was noted as representing the unity of the five elements, which included earth, air, fire, water, and spirit.

She continued shuffling through the pages and came upon the symbol notated as being the Sigil of Lucifer. On subsequent pages were odd drawings of demons fighting angels. A drawing of George surrounded by the message: *Die! Die! Die!*

And as disturbing as all these things were, she came upon a page that said: *I fooled her and she has no idea. How can someone love and hate another person so much? Confusion, confusion, confusion!*

Grace fell to her knees and sobbed. How could these things be true? "You need to get up," Zippora said. "I didn't fight this long and hard to get to you to see you give up that easily. You are childbearing and must do everything in your power to protect it. George is in terrible danger and you need to hurry to him now. I cannot assist you in what you must do. I have something I need to deal with."

Chapter 33

DISCLOSURE

Present day

Arya was sitting in the Devil's Chair, deep in thought. Devon was videotaping her, and Mila was inspecting the side of the chair where Arya had punched out the brick.

"You can't even tell it's there," Mila said.

"I had something happen to me last night that was so profound that it has really changed everything for me," Arya said.

"Is this why you woke us up so early this morning, demanding we come here?" Devon said. He looked at his sister through the camera's screen.

"I feel like I'm being ignored," Mila said.

"Here, I have something for you to do." Arya attached her phone to a selfie stick and handed it to Mila. "It's recording. Get the underside of the chair and make sure you film the ground and all sides of the chair as well. We need to see everything under there."

Mila took possession of the selfie stick, removed the bricks, and got to work.

"Do you want to share what happened?" Devon asked.

"You know the hotel that's here?" Arya asked, squinting against the bright Florida sun. "They built it after the first one burned down."

"OK."

"The one that burnt down was said to be due to faulty electrical wires. That's not an untruth, but there's a deeper reason behind it."

"And you know this, how?"

"It was shown to me." She took a moment before saying, "Very vividly. I saw the manipulation of the living, a spirit-guide escaping captivity, and how this area has been consumed in spiritual warfare since its inception. And, of course, I saw how the fire started."

"How did it start?"

"The spirit-guide I just mentioned? She manipulated the electrical wires to burn the hotel down."

"Why would she do that?"

"Incantations and spells were buried in the walls. She burnt it down to break them."

"That's insane," Mila said, her voice muted by the chair she was working in.

"What do you think this means?"

Arya shrugged. "That we're over the target. I think it also means I'm where I'm supposed to be and that I need to pay attention."

"To what?"

"I'm done," Mila said, then stood and brushed the grass and dirt off of her pants. "I got every inch inside that box. In fact, I did it twice."

"Thank you," Arya said. "I think we should go review the footage. I think we're about to find that out."

Chapter ③④

ORENDA

The past

"We have an alarming turn of events," Odious said as he came into the darkened room, out of breath. "I got here as fast as I could to tell you that the hotel is on fire, and the way it's burning, it appears as though the entire structure will be destroyed."

Zippora allowed the darkness to conceal her identity, hoping to use the element of surprise to her advantage.

"If it hasn't done so already," Odious said, moving into the room, still winded. "The binding spells used to control Zippora will break and free her. You can expect her to come looking for her directee. You must take a stand and keep her from getting to Grace. That means you must fight her to the death, if that's what's necessary. We need some time to allow Clyde to finish his directives and get out of here."

Zippora began to pace and nodded her understanding to buy as much time as possible and gather as much as she could to thwart their plans.

"Did you hear what I said?" Odious asked, his irritation growing much quicker than Zippora expected. "And why the hell are you standing in the dark?" Odious turned on the light, and when he saw Zippora was in the room with him, he looked at her with stunned disbelief. Discarded in the corner of the room was the lifeless body of the demon he had possess Grace. Her body was twisted and broken. By the time he moved his attention back to Zippora, she was already upon him.

She struck him in the face hard, sending him staggering backward. "Your attempts to exile me have filled me with an insatiable need for revenge, Odious!"

Odious tried to gain his footing and lift his defenses as Zippora came in with a second barrage of punches and kicks. He was successful at blocking around half the attacks, and ran to put distance between the two of them.

"Run all you want," she growled, her knuckles bleeding and her opponent's face raw. "This ends with only one of us walking out of here. Like your lackey over there, I will make sure you can never do this again."

She threw a wild punch, trying to deliver a knockout blow, but Odious feigned and ducked, avoiding her attack. He countered, throwing a haymaker of his own. His fist made contact with her exposed chin, and a loud smacking sound filled the room.

"Is that so?" he mocked.

Zippora shouted out in pain and fell, her head dizzy. Odious descended on her and unleashed a fury of punches of his own. She yelled out in desperation and tried to fight back. But he was much bigger and stronger, and he'd wounded her, placing her in a dire fight for her life.

When a blow struck her temple, her head filled with stars and her vision began to fade. That's when she heard Odious shout out in pain and his weight lifted off of her.

"You'll never harm a hair on her ever again," a strong male voice declared, and what followed could only be described as a crack of thunder.

Zippora's vision returned, and standing before her with an extended hand was a pleasant-faced American Indian. He wore a loincloth, leggings, and a shirt. His headdress featured an eagle feather standing straight up, and he had moccasins on his feet. In the opposite hand he held a spear wrapped in leather, detailed with beadwork and fur, the menacing tip made from carved bone.

"I am Seneca. George Colby is my directee. Take my hand," Seneca said.

Zippora pointed at Odious, who was getting to his feet. "He's . . ."

"Facing permanent banishment and he knows it," Seneca said, showing no worry about Odious and his speedy recovery. His hand remained out and patience surrounded him. Zippora took his hand and was pulled to her feet.

"George?" Zippora asked, her face swollen and bleeding from the scuffle.

"I warned him about Clyde's intentions," Seneca said. "It seems our plans on this side and theirs have intersected. Now, step behind me and let me deal with this demon once and for all." Zippora did and Seneca aimed his spear at Odious. He held it in a way as not to throw it, but to secure it from coming out of his grasp. "My orenda will easily take care of him."

And, as if it waited for him to finish speaking, the spear shot out a blue light with a thunderous crack, hitting Odious and consuming him until he was reduced to cinders.

Chapter ③ ⑤

MUTUAL UNDERSTANDING

Present day

"We need to speak about what happened," Devon said. "Ignoring it won't make it go away for either of us."

"There's no point," Arya said, shrugging. She wouldn't look at her brother sitting across from her at the table. "You have your point of view and I have mine."

"I hear what you're saying, but I don't think it's that simple. We have to talk about it."

"Well, there is another difference of opinion we have. I don't think it's complicated at all." She drummed her fingers on the tabletop. "By the way, how do you like my apartment?"

A thick silence wedged itself between the siblings and threatened to boil tempers.

"It's nice," he said, looking around. "I like it, and I think you were right. You are better off here."

"Can we get back to reviewing evidence or just ignoring each other?" She sucked her teeth. "I think it's better that way."

Devon sighed. "Look, Arya, I have some things I need to say. I don't know if it will make a difference or not, but please at least give me a minute."

Arya pursed her lips and settled into the seat, her focus finally finding her brother.

"What happened to you was wrong. I'm sorry I wasn't there for you the way I should have been. I should have listened and trusted you, but

I didn't." Devon stood and paced. "I really wish that I wrote down all the things I wanted to say. But I didn't because I would still be writing."

He stopped, looked at Arya, and said, "I don't want you getting mad, and I swore to Mila I wouldn't tell you, but you need to know the truth." He closed his eyes and resigned with a sigh. "Mila told you that she called me to go on the investigation. Something about needing my help. That's not exactly the truth. I called her and asked her to help. The way things ended that day, the way Mom spoke to you was devastating. I'd lost Dad, and I felt like I lost you too."

He sat, his eyes welled with tears. "What you said to me that day was true. I experienced it once and it freaked me out. I was looking for an easy answer when there wasn't one. I found a way to blame you, and it was easier than believing all of this stuff we're discovering to be true. But if anything good came out of it, it is this. We have a shared interest, mine spawned by a single experience and yours spawned by many. Maybe it can help us understand what was happening to you. And maybe we can help others."

He wiped his eyes. "I'm sorry. For whatever it's worth, I'm as sorry as someone could ever be."

Arya reached across the table and grabbed Devon's hand. "Thank you for that. It means a lot. How is Mom?"

He smiled and then shrugged. "I don't know. Why would you care? After you moved out, I got into a huge fight with her and left. The anger I felt over what she did to you and Dad came to a boil. She was wrong, Arya. For what she said and did, and I don't know if I can ever forgive that."

"The things you just told me were all I ever wanted to hear you say," Arya said.

"When I left the other day after we discovered the sledgehammer head at the graveyard, I mentioned I had somewhere to be. Do you remember that?"

"I remember."

"I made contact with Dad. I figured if I can't repair our relationship, then I can try and repair the one with our father."

"You what?" Arya felt a lump form in her chest. It was big and full and felt like it was going to explode.

"He wants to see you."

"Dad does?"

Devon nodded. "He told me how Mom made him stay away. How he hoped to hear from us one day when we were old enough to figure things out."

"I want to see him," Arya said as she started to cry.

Devon took out his cell phone and dialed. He pressed the device to his ear, paused, and said, "It's OK, Mila."

Moments later, there was a knock on the door. Devon looked at his sister and said, "You might want to get that."

"Devon?" she said, her face showing her state of confusion and concern.

"It's OK," he said. "I'll come with you."

He took her hand, walked her to the door, and said, "Mila and I brought him here with the expectation of you wanting to see him. You're not going to believe where he lives."

"Where does he live?"

"In Cassadaga, less than a mile away from the chair. He's a part of the spirit camp. He's a sensitive just like you."

Devon opened the door and, waiting on the other side, was her father. He opened his arms and said, "Arya," before hugging her tight.

Chapter ③ ⑥

ONE FINAL ACT OF BETRAYAL

The past

Clyde hated the fact that the moon was full. It lit everything up bright enough that objects cast significant shadows. Even at this time of night, if anyone was watching, they could easily identify him.

He leaned against the trunk of an old oak tree as he contemplated whether he should continue with his plan or simply wait for another, more opportunistic time.

"No," he reasoned with himself. "Odious was desperate and it appears as though I've run out of time. I must act now."

He looked upon the houses he had helped build and the smoldering pile of ash that was once the Cassadaga Hotel. It provided a steady flow of income to help the spirit camp flourish, and flourish it did. He felt a sense of pride in the things they'd accomplished as a community and the reverence associated with it. And for a brief moment, he mourned what he had to give up.

Yes, he cared for the people here. George was a genuinely good person who cared deeply about others. And there was Grace. His beautiful wife had a profound sense of innocence and a care for others the way only a mother could have.

But George was merely in his way. A piece on the chessboard that needed to be removed. Of course, his absence would slow the spread of his plight, giving Clyde and Odious a chance to instill their influence and will a bit easier.

In recognizing these things, he realized he couldn't harm Grace because, although he didn't mean to, he had fallen in love with her. Deeply. And because of the things he had to do now, he knew he could never face her again.

So, checking his surroundings one last time, once he was satisfied he wasn't being watched, he grabbed a piece of discarded lumber that could be used as a club and made his way into George's house. Clyde had an advantage. He had helped build the house, move the furnishings inside, and because of that, he was intimate with every inch of the layout.

Once he was inside, he moved through the darkened house and used the moonlight that penetrated the breaks in the window coverings to navigate the room. He could see the bedroom door was slightly ajar.

Tiptoeing to the open door, he gently pushed it. Slowly, it revealed more of the room, increasing his ability to scrutinize the space. Everything was as he remembered it, with the exception of the lump under the covers which was no doubt where George slept.

In response to these discoveries, Clyde's hand tightened around the handle of the club he held. He raised it, ready and willing to strike with extreme force.

A far-off sound stole Clyde's attention, forcing him to pause and watch George's sleeping body with vested interest. If he woke up and saw someone standing just beyond the foot of his bed, it could potentially frighten him and force a scream. This most certainly would alert others to potential trouble and would bring him unwanted attention. The thought of attacking now, with swift rage, wrestled with the idea of waiting to make sure this was done right, so he decided to play it safe and wait.

The sound that was most likely a nearby animal calling into the night faded and, thankfully, didn't disturb George one bit.

Moving forward and settling beside the bed, Clyde noticed a jug of water likely taken from the spring and pine pitch used in George's continued treatment of tuberculosis. Grace probably brought him that. In a misplaced sense of pity, he almost wished he could've done this months ago so George wouldn't have had to endure the sickness the way he did. Being near death for so long took a lot out of him, and the way Grace fretted over his ailing condition took a lot out of her, too.

Lifting the club high above his head, he picked a spot where it would be quickest and least likely for a fight to ensue if he didn't deliver the killing blow, and he swung with all his might. The club came crashing down on what Clyde believed to be the side of George's skull, and it responded with a hefty crack.

Delivering repeated blows, he didn't stop until fatigue set in. He dropped the club and it clattered on the floor. Reaching a hand out, he pulled back the sheets only to discover bricks where the head would be, as well as positioned foliage that had been stuffed under the blankets to mimic the shape of a body.

Cough.

Ripped from his confusion and surprise, Clyde's focus moved to the sound of the cough that was easily recognizable as having come from George, and to a closet on the other side of the room.

"You almost got away," Clyde said, taunting.

When he got to the closet, he opened the door to find George sitting with his back pressed against the wall, and a heavy layer of sweat covering his face. George wielded a kitchen knife, held at the ready.

"Now I know why Seneca couldn't get a reading on you," George said. He looked at Clyde with wide eyes, the pain of betrayal obvious in his stare. "You had the protection of a demon."

"The animal sound is what ruined your plan," Clyde said with fake comfort. "If I hadn't been delayed, I would have been out of here a minute or two before, thinking you had fled. I wouldn't have known you were hiding there, holding in a cough. You would have been free of me as I was on my way to who knows where."

"I don't understand why you did everything you did?"

"The things I did were used as cover and to build trust, George. You sensed something was off but couldn't put it together. Don't feel bad. I had a mission to complete and failure wasn't an option. It has taken me years, but it is done."

"So what's next then?" The knife George held shook. "A fight to the death instead of us living happily ever after in the community we built?"

"Like you, I've forever changed this place. You and I both know that even though you're much better, you're in no condition to fight me."

"I don't disagree," George said, holding a hand out to protect himself in case Clyde decided to attack. Then he stood. "But I'm not the type to just lay down and die. I don't suppose there is an easy way out of this for me?"

Clyde shook his head. "I'm afraid not."

"And what of Grace? What have you done to her?"

"I don't want to talk about Grace. You and I have something to settle, and if it ends up in my favor, you won't know the difference anyway."

Clyde took a step forward and feigned a lunge. George sliced the air with the knife, grunting as he did so.

"I have to ask," Clyde said with a devious smile, maintaining a threatening posture. "How did you know I was coming?"

"I thought I taught you better," George said, shaking his head. "Every day we learn something new. You should stop and listen." He paused, closed his eyes, and put a hand to his ear. "I want you to tell me what you hear."

Clyde did as George said, but he didn't hear anything. His smile vanished, and that's when he realized his connection to Odious had been severed.

"That means . . ."

"Zippora and Seneca figured it out," George said, dropping to the floor. "And that means your guide is—"

Grace heard Clyde and George talking, and by the sound of things, George was at Clyde's mercy. That's when she carefully and quietly picked up the heavy steel plaque intended to be attached to the outside of the hotel, commemorating the completion of the build. Her heart was pounding something fierce and her adrenaline was high. The heavy weight of the object she held was a bit lighter at that moment.

Slinging the object over her shoulder, she moved with haste but careful to be discovered. Entering the bedroom, she saw Clyde in front of the closet and George within.

"I want you to tell me what you hear," George said from the closet.

Clyde was in front of him, blocking any chance George had of escape. Considering the lingering effects of George's illness, she doubted he could fight off the much younger and more aggressive Clyde.

"That means . . ."

"Zippora and Seneca figured it out," George said, making eye contact with Grace as he dropped to the floor. "And that means your guide is—"

Grace lunged forward and swung the heavy plate into the back of Clyde's head. He fell to the floor in a heap. "Dead, you son of a bitch," she said, then dropped the plaque. She hurried to George and helped him stand.

"Come on," she said, her voice rising in panic. "We have to get out of here in case he gets up."

Grace and George exited the house and spilled into the moonlight-drenched night, seeking the help of other members of the community.

Chapter ③④

ARYA'S ELEGANCE

Present day

Arya was walking a path in a forest carved by thousands of footsteps. She could see a yellow house in the distance that had an empty rocking chair on the porch. There was no lady there or demons hiding in shadows waiting to attack. Instead, there was a feeling of tranquility. The setting she was in felt older than the now she lived in, and she knew she was in a connected vision that combined both the past and present.

As she journeyed along the path, she drew closer to what she recognized as the spring George used to heal the tuberculosis that plagued him for so long. Beyond the spring was Lake Colby, and standing at the shoreline of the lake was a woman who wore a dress and watched the rising sun burning away the thick fog that hovered above the water.

Arya walked to her, and they stood in a long, perfect silence that didn't require interference. Everything about it was soothing, the visuals stunning, and her nearness to the woman at the lake was like being with a long-lost family member.

"You did good," the woman finally said, not turning to look at Arya. She didn't need to. What was taking place was an enduring connection that defied expression.

"Yeah," she agreed. "You did, too, Grace."

Arya didn't ever want to leave this moment. There was such a strong sensation of belonging and peace with both Grace and the land. It was the closest thing to what Arya thought heaven might be like. "Did you live in that house?"

"I did," Grace said, and Arya could hear the delight in her response. "Among other places throughout the community as things were being built. But that house was my favorite, and I'm glad I got to see it again. The events I had to show you were distressing, and for that I am sorry. But I had to encourage you to see."

"Don't apologize." She reflected on the woman on the porch and the way she was attacked. "That incident on the porch. I'm not sure what I was being shown. Is that how you died?"

"No," Grace said. "That was a representation of the betrayal I felt from Clyde."

"I'm sorry you had to go through that." Arya drew a deep breath, the scent of pine strong. She exhaled and a natural smile spread across her lips. "It's beautiful here."

"All the more reason for evil to target it. To them, everything must have a stain on it." She sighed. "The things you went through when you were younger were by design. Nefarious players look to corrupt and interfere, always twisting things to their advantage and gain. When George and I returned with others to take Clyde into custody, he was gone. The only thing that remained from that incident was a bloodstain on the floor. I knew he would be up to his old tricks, and I've made it my mission to defy him every step of the way. I look forward to seeing him again soon."

Arya looked at Grace. "You are unbelievably strong and brave."

"As you are," Grace said, reaching out a hand. Arya took it. "The things that tormented you when you were younger were part of a scheme to get you to reject your gifts. To stifle them, shun them, and to pack them away and to never feel the need to develop them. It was my purpose to make sure that didn't happen."

"I'm glad you didn't."

"Those who oppose the goodness of our deeds didn't want this meeting to happen."

"I was frightened," Arya said, shuddering. "I didn't understand what was happening and felt so alone."

Grace squeezed Arya's hand reassuringly. "The idea that you're different from others is scary enough. Then, include the negative experiences you were having, and it creates the perfect storm of critical self-examination, anger, and rejection."

Arya looked to the lake, the fog much thinner now. A cool breeze touched her skin and lifted her hair. "That was you in the picture, wasn't it? That day I went to the chair with my friend?"

Grace nodded. "It was. I want you to know that I never meant to frighten you." She paused in silent contemplation. "The last thing I want to do is cause you more grief than you have already experienced, but I needed to get your attention."

"I understand."

"Gathering energy where I exist in order to manifest on the plane where you exist is difficult. Couple that with the timing needed with a dash of hope that when I make the big push to be seen, that the person I'm looking to gain the attention of is looking in the right direction and at the right time."

"I mean, I think I really understand." She smiled and felt proud. "You're my guide, aren't you?"

"I am."

Although the things she was being told were profound and complicated, Arya nodded her acceptance of what she was being told. "The chair?"

"Incantations used to lure people in so their energy can be used to allow the supernatural to come alive. Good and evil have always been at odds with each other. How does one create and destroy?" She folded her arms across her chest. "The use of energy. It's a simple concept, but a brilliant one. The innocent, the curious, and even the ornery are unsuspecting victims in the desires of the villainous souls that look to tip the scales in their favor. They will and always have used every trick in the book to gain the upper hand."

"And you?" Arya asked. She looked at Grace. "There had to be a reason why you were so determined to get my attention."

"I'd been waiting a long time for you to come along and for an opportunity such as that to present itself. I wasn't going to let that pass me by."

Arya took in a deep breath and exhaled with a huff. "Wow," she whispered. "I'm trying to wrap my head around this."

"Many who have come here are oblivious to this war and are trying to tame an innocent curiosity. Others provoke and look for proof of otherworldly things, sometimes getting responses they wish they'd never gotten. All of these scenarios, and many others, create energy that feeds the people on my side, creating an infinite loop of good versus evil."

"But why? What's the point?"

Grace shrugged. "I've come to accept that the push and pull of such things are embedded into existence itself. What path you choose to embrace is your own, and that is what shapes what side you're on."

"So where do we begin?" Arya asked.

"We place a sealing incantation that will mute their symbolism, and we start where you left off—at the chair. Once that's done, we move on to the next remnant."

"Only for them to come in behind us and undo what we're doing?"

Grace smiled. "You already understand."

Pictured is the Devil's Chair as I arrived on my initial visit to the Lake Helen Cassadaga Cemetery. If you look at the seat, you will see someone left a beer behind for the devil to drink.

Sitting off to the right of the Devil's Chair is George Colby's unassuming headstone.

Commemorative plaque

It is an understatement to call Lake Colby beautiful. Absolutely breathtaking. Remember, if you visit Cassadaga and the Devil's Chair, please be respectful.

Colby Memorial temple which is used for religious services, healing sessions, and spiritual lectures. The temple was built in 1923.

COMING SOON
FROM KEITH ROMMEL

* * *

PRE ORDER NOW

* * *

DELICATELY DISTURBED

Chapter ①

SLOWDOWN

Billy Frost gripped the steering wheel and stomped on the gas pedal. The engine revved and the car lurched as it picked up speed. A devious smile spread across his lips. "I see an open spot up front and it's ours!"

"Slow down," Evie-May said from the passenger seat. Her body moved with the car as it swayed, and she tried to resist the force. The hold she had on the grab handle was so firm that her knuckles were white, and her eyes were wide with concern.

"There's no need to worry," Billy said as he looked at his wife. "You're overreacting. It seems you've forgotten, I'm a professional."

"This isn't the best way for you to be advertising the business," Evie-May said, the tension in her voice rising over the growling sound of the engine. "I swear to God, I hate it when you act like this!"

"Relax," Billy said, weaving the sedan through the parking lot, cutting across spaces. Apparently, the white lines that sectioned out the parking lot were something for him to ignore. "It's just a little shortcut. Besides, I think you're really cute when you actually show you can be vulnerable."

"I don't like this," she said, hating to sound like a stick in the mud, but nothing about it was even remotely funny.

Billy's focus remained firmly on the parking spot closest to the entrance of the store. He guided the car with precision and swung left and then right so he could slide it into the open parking spot with ease.

"You see?" He lifted a brow and smirked as he put the car in park. "What you don't know is that I called ahead and had them reserve the spot for us. The rest of that was to show off my unparalleled skills."

"Yeah, sure," Evie-May said, her hold remaining firmly on the grab handle. "Wonderful."

Billy killed the engine and unbuckled his seatbelt. "Now, let's get going, time's a wastin'," he said before he kicked the door open and climbed out of the car. He looked inside the vehicle, and said, "Are you coming?"

"Yes," Evie-May breathed, willing her hand to release the stranglehold it had on the grab handle. Her forearm hurt and her hands were clammy.

"What the fuck do you think you're doing!"

Evie-May turned and saw a red-faced man approaching Billy with his hands waving in the air.

"Are you trying to kill someone, you moron?"

"What?" Billy said, facing the man.

"You're a damn idiot," the man said, spit flying out of his mouth and his face bright with rage.

"No, wait. Hang on a second," Billy pleaded, his hands up in case he needed to defend himself. "Calm down. I was just messing around and meant nothing by it. I'm sorry."

"Are you fucking kidding me? You're playing at the expense of other peoples' safety? You're unbelievable."

"No," Billy said as he shook his head. "I was paying attention and could see clearly that no one was around. Except right here in front of the store, the parking lot is practically empty."

"You're arrogant, too. What you were doing was speeding and cutting across the parking lot like it was a damn freeway, driving like a maniac!" The man was now standing dangerously close to Billy, his fists clenched. *This actually might get physical.* Evie-May fumbled around as she tried to unbuckle the seatbelt. "I should punch you right in your face to teach you a lesson!"

"Hey!" Evie-May yelled from inside the car. "You need to calm down!" She finally got her seatbelt off.

"I need to calm down? Who the hell are you?"

"That's my wife," Billy said, sounding pitiful.

"So you're a pansy, too. One that doesn't mind putting his family in danger and lets women fight his battles."

"I told you I was watching where I was going. I wasn't putting anyone in danger and I don't need someone else to fight my battles."

Evie-May hurried around the car. This guy Billy had pissed off was big and scary. Unlike Billy, it was obvious he had been in a number of fights throughout his life. A scar across his right eye accented the marble white eye that occupied the socket. He had a crooked nose which reinforced the impression that he was a scrapper.

The man shoved Billy. "Bullshit. You didn't even see me pulling out of my spot. You almost hit me!" The man pointed at his car. It was a silver something, idling with the door open. "What if my wife and kids were in there, you dumb shit!"

"Dude, keep your hands off of me. I already apologized to you."

"What you do is make excuses and think it's a damn joke." The man reached out and grabbed Billy by the shirt. He shook Billy violently. Evie-May tried to work her way between the two men.

"Stop it!" Evie-May shrieked but was shoved aside as the men began to tussle.

"Hey!" another man that was sprinting across the parking lot shouted. "Break it up, guys."

"Please help," Evie-May said.

The third man reached Billy and the Angry Man. He slid between the men. "I said to break it up!"

The Angry Man let go of Billy and pointed at the magnetic signs on the side of Billy's vehicle. "This guy is a driving instructor?" He put his hands on his hips and laughed. "You've got to be kidding me!" He took out his phone and took a picture of Billy and then the sign.

"I think you've made your point," Evie-May said to the Angry Man. "I really think you should go now."

"Is that so?"

"Yes, it is so." She looked at Billy then back at the Angry Man. "You're right. He was driving recklessly and I was telling him that while doing so. And I agree. It was dangerous and nothing about it was funny."

"I'm Parker," the third man said. "What's your name?"

"Billy."

"Well, Billy, I saw the way you were driving and I was wondering what the heck you were doing, too. I might've had a few choice words for you under my breath. This parking lot isn't the Daytona Speedway. Why don't you do the right thing and tell this man you're sorry."

"I already did."

"Say it again and this time with a bit more sincerity."

Billy nodded. "I'm sorry, OK? I was acting like a teenager and I'm embarrassed. I didn't think it would turn into this. I'm sorry."

"I didn't believe you when you first said it, and I don't believe you now," the Angry Man said. "From the sound of your voice and the stupid look on your face, it doesn't take a genius to know that you're a smartass and a self-centered prick."

"Hey man," Parker said to the Angry Man. "What's your name?"

"Ain't your fucking business," he said, turning his ire toward Parker. "And none of this was your concern to begin with. You should be careful inserting yourself into other people's business."

"Maybe it's not my business, but I think cooler heads need to prevail here, yeah? So let's all act like adults. With all due respect, I'll ask again, what's your name?"

"Tommy."

"Listen, Tommy, he said he was sorry. It was sincere enough, I think. And I agree with the lady. You've made your point. How about we declare this guy a moron, asshole, or whatever your words of choice are and just get on with our day?"

"Jeez, thanks a lot," Billy whispered.

Tommy nodded and stood tall as he pointed at Billy. "Your info is going online. People are going to know how you drive and behave. Good luck getting clients for your driving school. And lady, if I were you, I'd drive this idiot home so he doesn't hurt anyone—including you."

Tommy turned around and stormed off as the three of them watched him get into his vehicle and drive away.

"Thank you," Evie-May said to Parker. "I appreciate you stepping in."

"No problem," Parker said.

"I had it under control," Billy said, this time his voice loud enough for others to hear.

"Are you kidding right now, Billy?" Evie-May said. "Seriously, just learn how to read the room."

"And here I thought you were having a breakthrough moment and you learned some sort of lesson. Maybe you could at least be humble enough to pretend like you did," Parker said as he shook his head. "By the way, you're welcome."

"Yeah, thanks," Billy said again as he walked away.

"I'm sorry," Evie-May said, then she started after Billy.

"You embarrassed me and yourself," Evie-May said. Her face was red and her unblinking eyes bore a hole into Billy. "And then you insult the good Samaritan who tried to help you." She sighed. "What's going on with you?"

"Ev," Billy said.

"Don't 'Ev' me," Evie-May said. "Let's pick up what we came here for and get home. And yeah, I'll drive."

"Yeah, OK," Billy said, following her toward the entrance of the store.

"I'm really upset with you Billy."

"I can tell and I heard you, Ev."

"If you're going to do stupid stuff, do it when I'm not around and don't have the business signs on the car. It's careless. The last thing we need to do is to start screwing up what we worked so hard to build."

Billy walked in silence. Soon, he said, "You stress out all day at work. You have a bleak, difficult job. I was just trying to have a little fun with you, you know? Make you laugh at goofy crap. I didn't mean it to—"

But it did and look what happened! If you didn't notice, no one is having a good time right now. Not me, you, or the other guys. You took a dump on my only day off, and you better hope that guy doesn't give the school a negative review. If he posts details of what happened here today, it'll be devastating."

"He won't."

Evie-May stopped and spun on her heel. "Oh my gosh, you're so infuriating right now!"

"I'm just stating a fact. He won't."

"How can you be so sure?" The rage in her eyes was turning into disappointment. "You don't know that, Billy. You think you do, but you don't."

Billy shrugged. "He's a guy. He confronted me and got to shove me around a little bit. The big scary man wanted to rattle me, that's all. Mission accomplished. It's over."

"I hope so," Evie-May said. "For the sake of the school, I really do."

"Listen, I'm sorry that happened. I don't know what else I'm supposed to say."

Evie-May gave into her frustration and gave Billy a playful shove. "I don't want to fight all night, so let's drop it."

"Me neither and agreed." Billy put his wrists together. "Are you going to put cuffs on me, Detective Frost?"

"Believe me, I'm thinking about it."

"Ooh, that sounds like fun!"

To order this title, please visit:
www.keithrommel.com